GOOD AND EVIL IN BONANZA CITY

Rory Darson—A cold bounty man, he brought his prey in dead or alive. He risked his life for profit. Would he risk it for a town or for a woman's love?

Hannah Campbell—Caring, strong-willed, she was a mother to her younger sisters. Would she ever be a wife to Rory Darson?

Sonora Pike—As mean as a rattlesnake, twisted and perverse. Most men needed killing, Sonora figured. They were luckier than his women.

Natalie Ingram—Strikingly beautiful, strikingly cruel. She had sold her soul to the Devil to feed her dark obsession—with Sonora Pike.

Buck Campbell—A veteran lawman, he looked forward to hanging up his guns. Retirement would be sweet, he knew, if he lived to enjoy it.

Vern Simmons—An ambitious deputy, he wanted the sheriff's job—almost as much as he wanted the sheriff's daughter.

The Stagecoach Series
Ask your bookseller for the books you have missed

STAGECOACH STATION 35:

BONANZA CITY

Hank Mitchum

Created by the producers of
**Wagons West, White Indian,
Badge,** and **Winning the West.**

Book Creations Inc., Canaan, NY · Lyle Kenyon Engel, Founder

BANTAM BOOKS
TORONTO · NEW YORK · LONDON · SYDNEY · AUCKLAND

STAGECOACH STATION 35: BONANZA CITY

*A Bantam Book / published by arrangement with
Book Creations, Inc.*

Bantam edition / May 1988

*Produced by Book Creations, Inc.
Lyle Kenyon Engel: Founder*

ISBN 0-553-27168-7

Published simultaneously in the United States and Canada

Bantam Books are published by Bantam Books, a division of Bantam Doubleday Dell Publishing Group, Inc. Its trademark, consist-
ing of the words "Bantam Books" and the portrayal of a rooster, is
Registered in U.S. Patent and Trademark Office and in other
countries. Marca Registrada. Bantam Books, 666 Fifth Avenue,
New York, New York 10103.

PRINTED IN THE UNITED STATES OF AMERICA

KR   0 9 8 7 6 5 4 3 2 1

STAGECOACH STATION 35:

BONANZA CITY

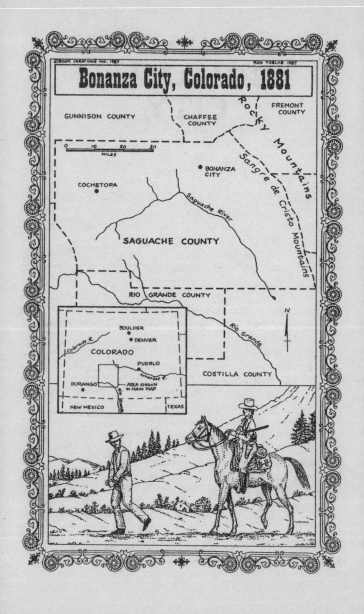

Chapter One

There was a cold wind in Rory Darson's face as he urged the horse up the rocky slope. The animal struggled with the rugged path, but he was game and not a quitter. Rory had never asked for more in a horse.

He sat easily in the saddle, swaying slightly. There was no indication that he half expected a bullet to come slamming into him at any moment.

The air was cold for spring, even here in the high Colorado mountains. It was April 1881, but Rory could not pin the date down any closer than that. He had been too busy chasing Sonora Pike to keep track of what day it was.

What mattered was that he had been on Pike's trail for better than three weeks; he was sure of that. And his belly was telling him, with every instinct that almost fifteen years of bounty hunting had developed in him, that the end of the pursuit was getting close.

Rory was a tall man, lean bodied, with wide shoulders that stretched the sheepskin coat he was wearing against the chill. His boots and saddle showed plenty of wear, like the battered broad-brimmed hat he wore. The holster and shell belt around his waist carried a long-barreled Colt with walnut grips worn smooth from use. He held the horse's reins in his left hand. His right gripped a Winchester '73, one of the finest rifles ever made as far as Rory was concerned. A man in his profession might stint on a lot of things and get away with it, but not on his weapons.

Folded up inside his saddlebag was the reward poster

on Sonora Pike. Rory had studied it by the light of enough campfires to have it all but memorized.

According to the poster, Pike was wanted for murder, robbery, rape, and assorted other villainies. The drawing of him showed a man with a broad face, small eyes, thick sandy hair, and enough scars for two men. There was a reward of five thousand dollars for his capture, dead or alive.

Rory Darson intended to collect that money.

Like Pike's face, Rory's also showed some battering. In fact, more than one person had taken him for an outlaw, just judging by his looks. He did not blame folks for coming to that conclusion. Maybe there was not that much difference between him and the men he hunted.

That thought had been occurring to him more often lately, and it was going through his head when he heard the flat *whap* of a bullet passing close by his ear.

Rory dug in his spurs, sending the horse surging forward along the narrow mountain trail. He heard the crack of a rifle, and then, after taking two steps, his mount suddenly stumbled. He felt the horse going down and kicked his feet free of the stirrups.

Rory dove desperately to the left as the horse went out from under him, falling to the right and rolling down the slope. The big bounty hunter knew he would have been crushed if he had not managed to leap off in time.

Rock chips stung his cheek as another slug smacked into the side of the hill near him. He jerked his head from side to side, trying to locate the rifleman. The weapon blasted again, and a fourth bullet kicked up dust between his feet.

Rory went down rolling, heading toward his horse, which was thrashing out its life a few yards down the slope, a bullet wound in its neck. Realizing that he had dropped the Winchester when he went flying from the saddle, Rory's eyes searched the ground, looking for it.

The horse stiffened and then lay still, and Rory saw the butt of the rifle sticking out from under its body.

Damn the luck! He had been afraid of an ambush and had been keeping the rifle in his hands to prevent just such a problem in case Pike shot the horse. Now the Winchester had gotten stuck under the animal.

Rory flopped behind the horse's body as a slug thumped into the carcass. It was the best cover—the *only* cover—on this cold, rock-strewn hillside.

It never entered Rory's head that his would-be killer might be somebody besides Sonora Pike. The outlaw had to know that a rider was on his trail. Rory had come within fifteen minutes of catching up to him in Pueblo, and he had been close a time or two since. Pike had been a hunted man for a long time and would know when someone was closing in on him.

Rory had the ambusher located now. Pike was farther up the hill, crouched among a clump of good-sized boulders. The outlaw had plenty of cover, Rory thought bitterly; all *he* had was a dead horse.

He reached over the body and tugged for a moment at the butt of the Winchester, but before he could pull it free another shot drove him back down. He rested his head against the still-warm belly of the animal and grimaced. Pike was out of range of the Colt.

That meant he had to get closer, had to leave what little shelter he had. There was no way around it.

Rory's long, supple fingers closed on the butt of the Colt and slipped it from its holster. He tensed his muscles, ready to make a dash for it . . . and wondered why he had been so damn stubborn as to ride into a likely ambush in the first place.

He had been warned. The sheriff in one of the little towns back up the line had told him, "Don't reckon there's a more cold-blooded bastard alive than Sonora Pike, son. He'll gun down anybody who gets in his way." The sheriff had looked at Rory for a long moment before adding, "Sort of like you, I reckon."

Rory had not taken it as an insult. He was used to people—especially lawmen—not liking bounty hunters. The way he saw it, he was just doing what most regular lawmen were not tough enough, or hard enough, to do. He had pitted his own abilities against some of the worst badmen in the West, and he had confidence in himself.

Which did not mean he was incapable of pulling some stupid stunts, he thought.

He launched himself from behind the horse, running hard to his right, stumbling slightly as small rocks rolled under his booted feet. He flipped the barrel of the Colt up and triggered off a couple of fast shots, knowing they were not going to hit anything. Maybe they would distract Pike for a second or two, if he was lucky.

Something, probably a bullet, tugged at Rory's coat as he ran. Ahead of him was a slight outcropping of rock, and he dropped behind it when he reached it, knowing that it barely covered him. Dust drifted into his face, making him cough. Things were going from bad to worse.

He fired again at Pike's hiding place, heard a loud whine as the bullet ricocheted off one of the boulders. It must have come close to Pike anyway, because the outlaw had let out a yelped curse.

Rory was on his feet and running again while the boom of the gunshot was still echoing against the mountains rising around them. There were some scrubby bushes up ahead of him, their leaves just starting to unfold. One of the branches jerked, cut apart by a bullet, as Rory darted behind the scanty growth.

He was angling uphill now, to one side of Pike's position. If he could reach a point where Pike could not fire down at him, things might be a lot different. Rory knew he had been lucky so far. Pike's shots had come close, just not quite close enough. He could not count on that luck continuing.

Seeing sunlight flash on the barrel of Pike's rifle, Rory fired on the run, snapping his last two shots at the outlaw. He flipped the Colt to his left hand with practiced ease and reached behind him with his right, groping for more cartridges in the loops of the shell belt.

Suddenly, his left foot turned under him as he ran. Gasping at the abrupt pain, he tried frantically to catch his balance but was too late. He went sprawling on the hard surface of the hillside.

Glancing up, Rory saw Pike emerging from the protection of the boulders, an ugly grin on his face. Pike must have seen him trying to reload the Colt, because the outlaw laughed mockingly and said, "Reckon you're just plain out of bullets *and* luck, bounty man." He started to lift the Winchester he held to his shoulder to take aim.

Rory lurched to one side as the Winchester cracked, the slug whining past his head. His hand flicked underneath the sheepskin coat and came out with the revolver he carried tucked behind his belt. It was a Smith & Wesson .44 with a slightly cut-down barrel, making it easy to conceal. The short barrel hurt its accuracy over longer ranges, but that did not matter now. It was all he had left, so it would have to do.

He triggered the weapon twice and saw dust puff out from Sonora Pike's shirt. Pike staggered back a step, and Rory came up on his knees and fired again. This time Pike's hat went sailing off his head.

"Drop it!" Rory barked at the outlaw as he lurched to his feet, the .44 lined on Pike's head. Pike hesitated, looking for a moment as though he were going to lift the Winchester again and resume his fire. "I've got two left," Rory pointed out. "One of them isn't going to miss, Pike."

Pike's lips drew back in a snarl, but he let the rifle slip from his fingers and clatter to the ground.

"That's better." Rory moved closer to Pike and gestured at the big pistol holstered on Pike's hip. "Lift out that Remington with your left hand and put it on the ground. Then back off."

Pike started to reach across his body to draw the Remington as commanded, but he stopped and winced. Jerking the thumb of his right hand toward his left shoulder, he said, "You hurt me, you son of a bitch! Can't you see?"

Rory saw the bloodstain on Pike's thick flannel shirt, and quietly he said, "I see it. Don't rightly give a damn, though. Get that gun out."

Moving gingerly, Pike did as he was told, grumbling as he slid the pistol from its holster and then stooped to place it on the ground. "Goddamn hidden gun," he muttered. "What's the matter, bounty hunter? Can't you take a man fair and square?"

Rory waved his free hand, moving Pike away from the

guns. He stepped forward and picked up the Winchester and the Remington. "Fair and square?" His voice was cold and his face bleak as he repeated Pike's words. "Like you treated that little gal in Denver fair and square? All you did was slit her throat when you were through raping her."

Pike had nothing to say to that. He just stared hard at Rory, his hand still clamped to his injured shoulder.

Rory glanced down the hill at the body of his horse and felt a pang of regret go through him. The animal had had a good heart. It had deserved better than to be shot down by scum like Pike, leaving Rory without a mount.

Rory had already holstered his own Colt. Now he tucked Pike's Remington behind his belt where he usually carried the Smith & Wesson. With the Winchester in his left hand and the .44 still trained on Pike, he asked, "Where's your horse?"

Pike inclined his head toward the top of the hill. "Up there. Ain't gonna help you much, though. Damn beast is all played out. That's why I figured I'd better dust you off my butt."

"Well, come on."

The two men trudged toward the top of the hill, the weariness of the chase showing in both of them. When they came over the rise, Rory spotted the horse standing head down near a stunted pine. Its sides were still heaving, and its hide was dark with sweat.

"Rode him into the ground, didn't you?" Rory commented harshly.

Pike cast a sideways glance at him. "Somebody was chasin' me," he pointed out in a dry tone. "You gonna do anything about this shoulder of mine, or do you plan on lettin' me bleed to death?"

"Sure," Rory replied. "I'll do something about it."

As he slammed the barrel of the Winchester into the small of Pike's back, the outlaw cried out in pain, dropping to his knees. Rory planted his foot against Pike's shoulder and drove him to the ground. Moving quickly, Rory yanked a pair of handcuffs from his pocket and clapped them on one of Pike's wrists; then he jerked the other arm behind him and fastened it with the other cuff. Then he straightened up and said, "Roll over. You try to kick me and I'll shoot you in the knee."

Pike glared up at him. "You'd do it, too, wouldn't you?"

"Damn right."

Stooping next to the outlaw, Rory took his knife from the sheath on his belt and cut away the bloodstained shirt. The wound was not a bad one from the looks of it, messy but not life threatening. The bullet had plowed through flesh but missed bone. Pike had been lucky, Rory thought.

He ripped a piece from the tail of Pike's shirt and bound it over the wound to stop the bleeding, not worrying much about whether the bandage was clean. There was a rope hanging on Pike's saddle, and Rory used it to tie the handcuffed man to the little pine tree.

"You don't take a hell of a lot of chances, do you?" Pike demanded.

"Not if I can help it," Rory murmured. He headed back over the hill, going down the slope to the body of his horse. He grimaced in regret again at the sight of the glassy, lifeless eyes. Then he bent and stripped his saddle from the body, bracing it with a foot while he heaved the gear loose. He carried the saddle and his own Winchester back to where Pike was waiting.

Rory carefully placed his saddle on the ground and then went over to the outlaw's exhausted horse. The animal looked nervously at this stranger, but it was too tired to shy away. Gently, Rory patted its flank, speaking to it in a low, soothing voice.

Behind him, Pike asked angrily, "What are you doin' with my horse?"

Rory did not look around as he answered, "Man who treats a horse like this ought to be shot. We'll wait . . . see how the old boy feels in the morning."

"Then what?"

A hint of a grin passed over Rory's face as he turned around and looked at Pike. "You're asking a lot of questions for a man who's handcuffed and tied to a tree. Don't reckon you've got much say in the matter. But if you've got to know . . . we'll wait and see if your horse can travel after a good night's rest. If he can, we'll head for the nearest town where I can turn you over to the proper authorities. I'll ride. You'll walk."

"The hell you say!"

Rory ignored the prisoner's outburst and began to gather twigs and small branches from the scrawny trees nearby. He glanced toward the high mountains looming over them, where there was still plenty of snow. Since it was cool now in late afternoon, it would be downright cold by morning. They would need a fire.

He supposed the sunlight slanting across the craggy peaks was beautiful, but he never had much time to consider such things. Too many other things occupied his mind—like staying alive. One positive side to this case was that Pike was a loner and had always operated by himself in his depredations. At least Rory did not have to worry about a gang trying to rescue him.

"Hey, bounty man," Pike called. "You ever been through here before? You know where the hell you're goin'?"

"I've seen maps," Rory answered flatly. He looked to the north. "There's supposed to be a town up there. Place called Bonanza City. Lots of mining in the area, I hear."

Pike's face contorted in a sneer. "You'll never get me there alive."

Rory shrugged. "Bounty's the same for a dead man," he said coldly.

Pike said no more.

Chapter Two

The night was a cold one, all right, just as Rory had expected. He made a pot of coffee to go along with the beans and bacon for supper, and the strong, hot liquid helped to cut the chill. A part of him did not want to give Pike any, but neither did he want to listen to the outlaw's grousing. With the Colt ready in his right hand, Rory used his left to unlock one of the handcuffs and then stepped back quickly.

"All right, help yourself," he told Pike. "But don't get any foolish ideas."

"Ain't you gonna untie my feet?" Pike demanded.

"You don't eat with your feet." Again the hint of a bleak smile passed over Rory's face. "Although I reckon maybe an animal like you just might."

Pike glared at him and leaned forward to reach the food and coffee. His feet were still bound, the rope running to the trunk of the pine tree, severely limiting his mobility. That was the way Rory liked it.

Pike ate hungrily while Rory watched. When the outlaw was done, Rory fastened the cuffs again, being careful in case Pike tried anything. The outlaw's shoulder was still hurting him, and Pike complained bitterly about it, but Rory ignored him as much as he could.

It would be a long time until morning, but Rory knew he would not sleep much, if at all. It did not pay to take chances with prisoners, even wounded ones who were handcuffed and tied to a tree. In his line of work, carelessness usually got you killed.

He settled down with his back against another of the scrubby trees, positioning himself so that he could keep an eye on Pike without having to look through the flames of the small fire. The Winchester was ready on his knees.

Pike grinned at him. "You'll doze off, bounty man," he said smugly.

"I wouldn't count on it. And the name's Darson, Rory Darson. I don't cotton to being called that other."

"I'll remember that . . . bounty man."

Rory considered slapping Pike's jaw with the butt of his rifle, but decided it would be too much trouble. Instead, he said quietly, "I don't usually wait around for the hanging after I bring a man in. I might make an exception for you, Pike."

The outlaw snorted contemptuously but did not say anything else. He turned his face away from the fire and made himself as comfortable as he could, curling up awkwardly on the ground and hunching his shoulders against the cold night air.

The fire died down some as the night wore on. Rory fed more twigs into it from time to time, content to keep it a small blaze. As he leaned back against the pine, he slowly slipped into a quiet state that took the place of sleep. He was still awake and alert, but a part of his brain was resting. It was an ability he had developed out of necessity over the years.

What happened next was not really a dream, since he was not asleep, but a vision, the same dark and bloody image that had been haunting him for years whenever his mind relaxed too much.

He saw his mother's face, twisted in pain . . . his father, battered and broken . . . the bodies of his grandparents, casually slaughtered and flung aside . . . and his sister, the worst of all. God, the things they had done to her, and then after all of it, the monsters had left her alive to suffer and die alone.

She would have died alone, too, if her brother had not come galloping in, drawn by the smoke from the house,

his whiskey-soaked stupor blasted to bits by the horror he
was seeing. He arrived in time to take his sister in his
arms and feel the final shudder wrack her body, to see the
agony in her eyes—

Rory's head jerked up, his eyes wide and staring, his
finger tightening on the finger of the Winchester. He
eased off just in time to stop the rifle from blasting a slug
into the back of the sleeping Sonora Pike. Rory drew a
deep, ragged breath. Pike would never know just how
close he had come to dying tonight.

By dawn, the weather had changed, and a warm breeze
blew from the south. Rory shucked off his coat as he went
to check on Pike's horse. After being rubbed down, fed,
and watered the night before, the animal had looked
stronger, and now, after a night's rest, he was almost
frisky.

Rory patted him, grateful that the animal's recovery had
been this quick. He put his own saddle on the horse and
then walked over and roughly prodded Pike with a boot.
"Get moving," he said. "We've got some ground to cover
today."

Pike groaned and tried to raise up. "Hell! I'm all stiff
from sleepin' on that cold, hard ground."

"Better than sleeping in it," Rory commented. He set
the coffeepot back on the coals of the fire.

By the time the sun was up, he was ready to start
toward Bonanza City. Leaving Pike handcuffed, he slashed
the bonds on the man's ankles. Pike complained of the
stiffness in his muscles again, but he managed to get on
his feet.

Rory swung up into the saddle, keeping the muzzle of
the Winchester in his arms angled toward Pike. "Lead the
way," he ordered.

"Ain't fittin' for a bounty hunter to steal a man's horse,"
Pike complained. "You can't make me walk all the way
into Bonanza City. Shoot, it must be twenty miles."

"Reckon we'd better get started, then."

They moved out, leaving the ashes of the fire behind

them. The country was rugged, and the going was slow, especially with Pike on foot. As the sun rose, so did the temperature. The wind that tugged at their clothes was downright hot, and it was not long before Pike's shirt was soaked with sweat.

Rory called a halt at midmorning and gave Pike a drink from the canteen hanging on the saddle. They were in a spot shaded by pine trees, out of the glare of the sun. The vegetation here was a little more lush than it had been farther south.

"This shoulder of mine is startin' to pain something fierce," Pike said as he leaned against one of the pines. "I don't know if I can make it into town, Darson."

"You will," Rory replied flatly. His eyes were scanning the horizon. He had thought a moment earlier that he saw some smoke, and now he was trying to locate it again.

There it was, a thin spiral of gray against the blue of the sky. He followed it down, saw that it seemed to be coming from behind a ridge a couple of miles away. Might be a ranch, he decided, or some settler who was foolish enough to try farming in this country. Either way, whoever was over there might have an extra horse for sale.

Another horse meant that he and Pike would reach Bonanza City that much sooner. And that meant that the bounty on Pike's head would be in his pocket sooner.

"Come on," he said. "We're swinging over to that ridge over there."

Pike glanced in the direction Rory indicated and spotted the smoke. He nodded and began walking again, limping slightly. Rory knew how difficult it was for a man who was used to riding to have to walk in boots. Pike had to be hoping the same thing that he was, that there would be an available horse over that ridge.

When they topped the wooded rise forty-five minutes later, Rory reined in and studied the little clearing that was spread out beneath them. It was a pretty park with a trail running through it, and on the far side was a fair-sized cabin with a corral behind it. Several horses stood grazing in the corral.

A grin stretched Rory's face. "Stage station," he murmured. This was a stroke of luck. He had not known that they were heading for a stage line, let alone a relay station. From the looks of the trail, it would lead straight into Bonanza City.

Pike was smiling, too. "Looks like you won't get to make me walk all the way after all, bounty man. There'll probably be a stage along before long. We can ride in style."

"Could tie you to the boot and make you run along behind," Rory said dryly. "I'd just shut up if I was you."

Pike glared but did not say anything else as they moved down toward the stagecoach station.

When they were still a hundred yards away from the building, the door opened and a man stepped out holding a rifle. His bald head shone in the sunlight, and he had a bushy white beard. When Rory and Pike were a little closer, he called out, "That's far enough, mister. Who are you?"

Rory reined in, keeping both hands in plain sight. So far, he had not seen anyone else around the station. If the old man ran the place by himself, it was likely he was more than a little cautious, in addition to what was only sensible when strangers rode in.

"Howdy," he called back. "Name's Rory Darson. I'm not looking for any trouble."

The stationmaster jerked his beard in Pike's direction. "What about your friend?"

Rory shook his head as he replied, "He's not my friend. Prisoner I'm taking to Bonanza City."

"You a lawman?"

"Nope."

"Bounty hunter, then." The old man squinted and then suddenly stiffened. The rifle was not held so casually in his hands now. "Hell, that there's Pike."

"That's right, you old coot!" Pike shouted fiercely at him. "And if you know what's good for you, you'll blast this big ugly galoot with me and get me out of these cuffs!"

Still on his horse, Rory let Pike finish and then kicked him in the right shoulder, knocking him down. "If you're not careful, you'll hurt my feelings, Pike," he said mildly.

Raising his voice, he called to the old-timer, "This is Sonora Pike, all right. Don't look like much of a desperado now, does he?"

The old man laughed, and the barrel of his rifle dropped back toward the ground. "No, he sure don't. Come on in, son."

"On your feet, Pike," Rory ordered the outlaw.

Pike struggled up from the ground. The look he gave Rory was of pure hatred. "I'll kill you sooner or later, bounty man."

Rory ignored the threat and urged the horse forward. Its shoulder bumped Pike and started him moving again.

When they reached the cabin, Rory swung down from the saddle and nodded to the old man, who was still standing near the door. "You know if there'll be a stage through anytime soon?" he asked.

"Reckon you're lucky. The northbound's due at noon. It'll take you right on into Bonanza City." The stationmaster stuck out his hand. "Name's Glidden."

Rory shook hands with him. "Glad to meet you, Mr. Glidden. We'll wait for the stage, if that's all right with you."

"Long as you got money to pay for your tickets, son, it's all right with me." Glidden narrowed his eyes as he looked at Pike. "You reckon it's safe to let this feller run around loose?"

"He won't run," Rory promised. "Pike's got more sense than that."

Pike, saying nothing, continued to glare at Rory.

Glidden cradled the rifle in his arms. "You boys want something to eat? I was just fixin' some grub for the stage passengers."

It had been quite a while since the scanty breakfast that Rory had prepared. He said, "That sounds mighty good."

"Well, come on inside, then."

Rory and Pike followed the old man into the shadowy interior of the station and sat down at a long, rough-hewn table. Glidden went to a stove in one corner and dished out two bowls of the stew simmering in a big black pot. When he put the bowls down on the table, Pike complained, "How can I eat stew with my hands cuffed behind me?"

Glidden laughed again, obviously enjoying the outlaw's predicament. "Could put your face in the bowl and go after it like a pig does slop," the old-timer cackled.

Rory took the key to the handcuffs from his pocket and tossed it to the stationmaster. "Unlock the cuffs," he said as he slipped his Colt from its holster and drew back the hammer. He crossed his arms, leaning his elbows on the table and angling the pistol's muzzle at Pike.

Being careful not to get too close, Glidden leaned over and used the key on the handcuffs, unfastening the one around Pike's right wrist. The outlaw brought his hands in front of him, grimacing at the soreness of the muscles. "Damned inhuman contraption," he muttered.

"Eat," Rory said.

The stew was good. Both men enjoyed it, finishing what Glidden had given them and accepting his offer of seconds. Pike seemed to be on his best behavior, and gradually Glidden relaxed. But Rory kept a close eye on the outlaw, not wanting to give Pike any opportunity to make a break for freedom.

Glidden ate a bowl of the stew himself and then pulled out a large pocket watch. Flipping it open, he said, "It's past noon. Stage ought to be here soon. It's generally not more'n an hour late."

Rory took a small roll of bills from his pocket and tossed them up and down on his palm for a moment. His stake had shrunk quite a bit. It was a good thing he was going to be collecting that bounty on Pike. "What'll those two tickets to Bonanza City set me back?" he asked.

Glidden went to a battered desk in the opposite corner from the stove and consulted a chart to figure the price. He wrote up the tickets and took the money that Rory handed him. Rory glanced at the diminished roll of bills again and then stuffed them back in his pocket.

From the table, Pike asked, "You got any whiskey around here, old man?"

Before Glidden could answer, Rory shook his head. "No drinking."

"Why the hell not?" Pike demanded. "What's it matter to you?"

"Whiskey fires a man up, sometimes makes him think he can dodge bullets or that they won't hurt him if they do hit him. I don't want you thinking that way, Pike."

Pike grinned. "Like you said, that reward's the same dead or alive. Why are you so all-fired concerned about me, Darson?"

"I'd just as soon not waste any more shells on you," Rory drawled, and then he lifted his head as he heard the far-off blare of a trumpet.

"That'll be the noon stage," Glidden said, heading for the door of the station. "I'd best start gettin' that fresh team ready."

Rory and Pike stayed where they were as the stagecoach rolled up to the station a few minutes later. Rory watched through the open door of the building as the dust settled. Then he stood up and motioned with his Colt for Pike to follow him. He backed out into the yard, keeping Pike covered.

The driver and the shotgun guard had just hopped down from the box and were greeting Glidden when they spotted Rory and his prisoner. Both men frowned. "You got some trouble here, Glidden?" the driver asked.

The stationmaster shook his bald head. "Nope, just a bounty hunter. That there prisoner is Sonora Pike, boys. You've heard of him."

"Damn right," the young guard exclaimed. "He's wanted all over the territory!"

Pike glanced at Rory, who saw an unmistakable glint of pride and satisfaction in the outlaw's narrow eyes. He was famous, and it did not really matter to him that it was for some of the worst crimes Colorado had ever seen.

"You move and I'll waste one more shell," Rory warned him in a low voice. Then he stepped over to the driver and said, "Got room for two more, mister?"

The driver looked dubiously at him. "You've got tickets?"

"I've got tickets. For both of us."

"Then I reckon you ride. Can't say as I like the idea much, though." The driver glanced over at the guard, who was still staring at Pike. "You going to open that door for the folks, Harve?"

"Oh. Sure, Deke." The guard brought his attention back to the coach. "Right now."

He stepped over to the door of the stage and swung it open. As the first of the passengers climbed out, the driver said, "All right, folks, this is a meal stop. Go on inside. There's probably stew on the stove."

"There is," Glidden confirmed. He was beginning to unhitch the tired team.

Rory moved Pike back, out of the way of the disembarking passengers. A frown creased his lean features as he saw that two women were among them.

The first one off the stage was a woman in a dark blue dress, wearing a black hat that sported a feather in its band. Her clothes were rather dusty, but they were expensive and well made. Her hair was black and swept up in an intricate arrangement. Fine, delicate features were highlighted by eyes that were an even darker blue than her dress. Her eyes swept over Rory and Pike and did not seem even to see them.

The other woman was several years younger, in her early twenties, Rory would have said. She was quite a contrast to the first one. Her hair was a rich, lustrous red, worn in simple braids that were wrapped around her head. Rory imagined that when it was let down, it would be long and thick. He caught himself thinking that and gave a small, surprised shake of his head. Such thoughts did not usually occur to him. The girl's dress was clean and well cared for, but it was obviously homemade. It looked good on her.

A man climbed down from the stage and immediately joined the beautiful dark-haired woman. He was tall and almost painfully thin, with a short dark beard and eyes that seemed as unconcerned with his surroundings as his companion's had been. He wore city clothes and shoes, and there was a dapper derby perched on his head. As he stepped to the woman's side, she took his arm, and the two of them marched into the station.

Rory saw the man wince slightly as the woman's fingers

dug into his arm while they passed—probably because she was out of place here on the frontier and all too aware of it, he thought. Most city women were high-strung and could not take any kind of hardship, even that of a stage-coach ride.

The redheaded girl was not like that. Rory could tell that she was not bothered by the rough, dusty journey. She looked at him briefly and then went into the station behind the other woman and the man.

There were two other passengers, and Rory's experienced eye pegged them without any trouble. One was a drummer with a loud coat, concealing a flask from which the man probably took an occasional sip. The other man was young and wore spectacles and a very sober suit. Even if he had not been carrying a Bible, Rory would have known him to be a preacher. He felt a wave of dislike go through him as the minister walked by. Even as a boy, he had never had much use for soul savers and Bible thumpers, no matter how hard his parents had tried to thump some religion into him.

When the passengers were all inside the station and Glidden and the guard were busy changing the teams, Rory approached the driver and jerked a thumb at the top of the coach. "See you're not carrying anything up top," he said. "Reckon I could use it?"

The driver looked puzzled. "What do you want to put up there? Plenty of room in the boot for any bags you've got."

"I'm not talking about baggage." Rory nodded toward Pike. "I'm talking about him. I've got some chains in my saddlebags—"

Pike shook his head violently. "Oh, no, bounty man. You ain't gonna chain me, no, sir! You might as well just shoot me right now."

"Riding on top's usually not as dusty as inside," Rory pointed out.

"I don't care! I ain't gonna be chained!"

The driver nodded thoughtfully. "It might bother them women to have a cold-blooded killer ridin' inside with them," he said.

"That's what I thought," Rory agreed. Pike was cursing them heartily, his voice rising as Rory stepped closer to him. He put the barrel of the Colt against the bottom of Pike's nose, none too gently. "Shut up, Pike. I said I don't want you bothering those women, and that includes cussing."

Pike glowered as he fell silent. Rory backed up slightly and told the driver where to find the chains, and then he motioned for Pike to climb aboard the coach.

As he settled down on top of the stage, Pike said quietly, "Last time I broke out of prison I swore I'd never be chained again, Darson. I won't forget this."

"Don't reckon you will. Just put one more mark against me, Pike, for when we settle up later."

The outlaw suddenly grinned. "Oh, I will, bounty man. Don't you worry about that. I will."

Inside the station, the redheaded young woman, whose name was Hannah Campbell, had taken charge, finding bowls and ladling out the stew from the pot. She handed two servings to Stefan Kendrick, who carried the bowls over to the table and joined his traveling companion, Natalie Ingram.

Hannah winced slightly as the drummer—Calhoun, she thought his name was—came up to her with a smile. She could smell the whiskey on his breath as he took the bowl and said, "Thank you kindly, my dear." He had been watching her for most of the trip, and she did not like the lecherous thoughts she could read in his eyes.

Luckily, the preacher approached just then, and quickly Calhoun went to the table and sat down. Calhoun and the Reverend Mr. Longmire did not get along too well. The minister had not been shy about telling the drummer that his flask was a tool of the devil.

Hannah gave Longmire a bowl of stew and then took one for herself. She carried it to the table and found a seat at the end of one of the benches.

"Did you see those horrible men outside?" Longmire

asked from a few feet away. "I'm sure they were despera-
does."

Hannah smiled slightly. She knew that the minister was
from Philadelphia; he had been persistent in telling her all
about it. He was on his way to a new church in Wyoming,
and he frequently betrayed his lack of knowledge about
things in the West.

"I believe one of them was a lawman," she replied
quietly. "And the other one was his prisoner. You were
certainly right about that one, sir. A desperado if I ever
saw one."

"And I would imagine that being a sheriff's daughter,
you have seen plenty of outlaws."

"That's right, Mr. Longmire." Hannah smiled again,
but not at Longmire. She knew the man was interested in
her, and she did not want to encourage him. Even if she
had been attracted to him, she would not have pursued
him; she had too many responsibilities to get involved
with anyone, especially someone who was traveling on
past Bonanza City.

"Looks to me like a bounty hunter," Calhoun spoke up.
"He's chainin' that other fella on top of the stage."

Hannah frowned and looked through the open door of
the station. The drummer was right. The tall, rawboned
man had forced the other one to climb up on top of the
coach and even now was in the process of securing him
with chains to the railing that ran around the roof of the
vehicle. Outrage flared within her. That was no way to
treat a man, not even a criminal.

"My word!" Longmire exclaimed. "You're absolutely
right, Mr. Calhoun. They're treating that man like he's
some sort of beast!"

Definitely a bounty hunter, Hannah thought, her features stiff. She had been around lawmen all her life, and
they did not treat prisoners like that. At least her father
did not, and if there was a better lawman anywhere than
Buck Campbell . . . Well, there just was not, and that was
all.

"I think it's horrible," she said in a low voice.

If the bounty hunter heard any of the disapproving

comments through the station's open door, he gave no sign of it. No doubt he was used to it, being in such a brutal, mercenary profession.

And yet, Hannah thought, at first glance he had not seemed like such a bad man.

Stefan Kendrick and Natalie Ingram did not join in the discussion, nor for that matter, Hannah noted, did they even look out the door at what was going on in the station yard. That was no surprise. Other than introducing themselves and saying that they were going to Bonanza City, they had said very little during the trip. Both of them looked as though they would be more at home in a drawing room than in a bouncing stagecoach.

Hannah knew that what her companions did or did not do was none of her business. She was just anxious to get back home. She had been away for two weeks, helping her sister Alice, who had just had her first baby. Alice was younger than Hannah by two years, but she was already married and now was starting a family of her own.

Hannah should have been jealous of her sister's happiness, she supposed, but she had plenty to occupy herself. There were four more redheaded Campbell girls at home, plus their father, Buck Campbell, to take care of. Hannah was more mother than sister to the girls, especially since Faye Campbell had died giving birth to Emily, the youngest, six years earlier. Hannah did miss her mother, but life had to go on, and it seemed that she was the only one who could hold the family together. There would be time for her own life later.

She was musing on those thoughts when she became aware that the Reverend Mr. Longmire was still complaining about the way the bounty hunter was treating his prisoner. The drummer, Calhoun, joined in by spinning yarns about some of the other bounty hunters he had seen. "Hell, I don't know who's worse, the outlaws or the men hunting the rewards on them," he said.

In this case, Hannah thought, glancing through the door again, there indeed did not seem to be much difference.

*　　*　　*

When Rory had Pike secured on top of the stage and had tied the horse to the back of the coach, he sat down on a bench near the station door to keep an eye on the outlaw. As he leaned back against the log siding, he could hear snatches of the conversation coming from inside.

He heard enough to know that the passengers did not approve of him or the way he was treating Pike. That was just too damn bad, he thought as a slight smile played over his grim face. Those pilgrims did not know how dangerous a man like Pike really was. Taking any chances with him would be asking for trouble.

Rory did not intend to have any trouble on the way to Bonanza City. Although he had holstered his Colt, he kept his hand near the butt of it.

Sonora Pike sat on top of the coach, glaring murderously at him.

When the teams had been changed, the driver and the guard went inside for a quick bowl of old Glidden's stew. Rory waited, beginning to feel slightly drowsy in the hot sun.

The passengers emerged from the station a few minutes later. The stage would not leave for a short while yet, and they still had time to visit the outhouse behind the station or walk around and stretch their legs. As the dark woman and her companion came through the door, Rory felt her eyes on him and glanced up to meet her gaze. The intensity in the deep blue eyes surprised him, but he merely nodded to her. The woman's friend pressed her arm, and they strolled on toward the stage.

Rory felt a slight tightening in his belly. She was an attractive woman, and despite the fact that he tried to steer clear of any involvements, he had the same reactions to a pretty lady as any man.

He glanced over and saw that the redhead had come out of the cabin and was watching him watch the other woman. Rory saw the disapproval in her eyes and grinned. The girl did not like him, maybe because he had been looking at the other woman, maybe because he was a bounty hunter. Either way, Rory thought, it did not matter a damn to him.

Rory ignored the preacher, who was frowning at him, too. The drummer was not worth bothering with, either. It appeared that he was not going to have the most pleasant company on the trip to Bonanza City.

"All right, folks, we'll pull out in one minute," the driver announced as he and the guard came out of the cabin. "If you've got any more business, you'd best tend to it."

Rory waited until the other passengers had climbed aboard the coach. Then he grasped the edge of the door and stepped in. He saw that the two women and the tall man in city clothes had taken the front seat, which left him an empty spot next to the preacher on the rear seat. He sensed the man flinching away from him as he sat down.

As he settled into the seat, he looked up and met the eyes of the young redhead, who was directly across from him. Nodding his head, Rory said, "Howdy, ma'am."

"Hello," she replied in a soft voice, looking away.

"Name's Rory Darson," he went on, not sure why he was trying to be friendly to someone who had obviously disliked him on sight.

"I'm . . . Hannah Campbell."

Rory smiled. "Pretty name."

"Indeed it is." The drummer stuck his hand past the minister. "Orville Calhoun, my friend. Farm implements is my game, and I venture to say I know what yours is." When Rory shook his hand but did not say anything, Calhoun pressed on. "You're a man-hunter, aren't you?"

"Reckon you could call me that," Rory admitted.

Up on the box, the driver cracked his whip and the team surged forward. The stagecoach lurched into motion.

Clutching his Bible, the minister grudgingly introduced himself to Rory. "Albert Longmire," he said, not offering to shake hands. Rory nodded a greeting.

"I'm Stefan Kendrick," the tall man said. "This is Miss Natalie Ingram."

"Pleased to meet you, ma'am," Rory told the woman.

She regarded him solemnly for a long moment and then said in a deep voice, "Hello, Mr. Darson." There was a throatiness in her tone that was undeniably appealing, even though her words were flat and unemotional.

Rory saw the way Kendrick casually rested his hand on Natalie Ingram's and got the feeling that the two of them were more than traveling companions. He had to admit that in their city clothes, they appeared to be well matched.

The Reverend Mr. Longmire could hold in his outrage no longer. Gesturing toward the roof of the coach, he said, "Did you have to chain that man up there, Mr. Darson? It seems barbaric to treat a man like that."

Before Rory could reply, Hannah spoke up in agreement with the minister. "You were acting as if he were some sort of animal," she accused coldly.

Rory looked from Longmire to Hannah and left his gaze on her as he said, "Reckon he might as well be. That's Sonora Pike, Miss Campbell. You won't find an outlaw with bloodier hands anywhere in these parts."

"Sonora Pike?" Hannah clearly recognized the name. "I . . . I've heard of him."

"I don't care who he is. He's still one of God's creatures!" Longmire said, his voice rising as he warmed to his subject. "I suppose I should expect such behavior from a bounty hunter."

Rory looked at the preacher for a long moment from the corner of his eye, not surprised that Longmire was reacting the way he was. Some folks seemed to wear blinders when it came to outlaws, seeing only what they wanted to see. From time to time, he felt it was his duty to rip those blinders off.

"Well, sir," he said slowly, "I don't know about bounty hunters, but I can tell you what kind of behavior you could expect from Pike. If he was loose and you were in his way, he'd shoot you down like a dog. And as for what he'd do to these women here . . ."

Kendrick broke in. "Really, sir, I don't believe you need to go into detail—"

"He killed a little gal in Denver a couple of months ago," Rory went on, overriding Kendrick. "Fifteen she was, and Pike raped her. When he was through with her he cut her throat with a knife. Did the same last year to a twenty-year-old schoolteacher in Colorado Springs. He hit a bank over in Kansas, killed the folks working there, and then burned the building down around them. I could go on . . . if you want me to."

Longmire, who had paled during the recitation of Pike's crimes, shook his head.

Rory's voice was harsh as he concluded, "The way it seems to me, Reverend Albert Longmire, when you're drawing comparisons between Pike and an animal, you're insulting the animal. That's why Pike's chained up there."

He glanced across the coach and saw that Hannah had blanched, too. The fact that he had upset her bothered him a little, but she had come down on the preacher's side. Listening to the truth would not hurt her too much.

"I understand what you're saying, Mr. Darson," Longmire said. "But the Bible tells us to turn the other cheek."

Rory's lean cheeks tightened as he tried to hold in his anger. He told himself that Longmire did not know what he was saying. In deceptively soft tones, he said, "That's what my folks always believed. They were great ones for reading the Bible. Told me to turn the other cheek. Then one day when I wasn't at our farm, a bunch of renegades came riding by and thought the place looked like easy pickings. Reckon my pa tried to turn the other cheek, but if he did, they just kicked it in, too. They killed my folks, my grandma and grandpa, and my little sister, Reverend. Men just like Pike up there."

The drummer, who was taking in the story with an open mouth, took a quick nip from his flask when Rory paused and then asked, "What happened to those men, friend?"

"I found 'em," Rory said flatly. "Every last one of them. They were all wanted, so I guess you could say that was the beginning of my bounty-hunting career."

"How horrible for you," Natalie said quietly.

"Yes, ma'am," Rory agreed. "Now I hunt men like that for a living, but at least I take them alive when they'll let me. That's more than some can say."

Silence filled the coach as Rory's words died away. Hannah was still pale, and the Reverend Mr. Longmire looked slightly uncomfortable. Rory thought he should have been satisfied at the way he had set them straight, but he did not feel particularly good about it. All he had really done was dredge up bad memories.

Stefan Kendrick had not said anything else, and neither had Natalie Ingram. Rory saw now that she was still watching him, though. Her interest seemed to have grown. As his eyes met hers, a slight, seductive smile tugged at the corners of her full lips.

Rory did not return the smile. He had encountered women before who found his profession thrilling and attractive. Usually, they wanted to know how many men he had killed and wanted to know about all the crimes his prisoners had committed. He had no use for that type of woman, no matter how beautiful.

He looked out the window of the coach, watching the mountains and the trees through the dust kicked up by the wheels. He would be mighty glad to reach Bonanza City and get Sonora Pike off his hands.

Chapter Three

Laid out along the banks of Kerber Creek, in a broad valley between the Sangre de Cristo Mountains and the Cochetopa Hills, the hustle and bustle of Bonanza City gave no indication that the settlement had been in existence less than two years. The discovery of gold and silver in the valley had brought people flooding in. Mining camps had sprung up all along the creek, but Bonanza City had outstripped them all, growing so rapidly that residents had begun referring to it as the new Leadville.

With a population now of over thirteen hundred to look after, Sheriff Buck Campbell had over thirteen hundred headaches in that town alone, not to mention those caused by the other inhabitants of Saguache County. At least that was the way he saw it.

As he leaned against the hitch rail in front of the Bonanza City Emporium, waiting for the stage to arrive, he was thinking how good it would be to have Hannah back home. Watching over a county with a booming mining town was a big enough job without having to ride herd on four feisty redheaded daughters.

The girls were clustered on the boardwalk behind him, out of the afternoon sun. As he listened to their chatter and laughter, a good feeling spread through him. The girls had always brought him more pleasure than anything else in his life, and they sure did not give him the time to brood about anything in the past.

A solid, blocky man a little below medium height, Campbell had the same red hair that he had passed on to his children, just a whole lot less of it. When he took off his hat to mop sweat from his forehead, the sun glinted off his large bald spot.

The young man standing beside Campbell gave a mock wince. "Careful there, Buck," he warned. "What're you trying to do, blind me?"

Campbell jammed his hat back on and glared at Vern Simmons. "A blind deputy wouldn't do me no good, now would he?"

"No, sir, not much."

"Neither would one who talks more than he thinks," Campbell growled.

Vern grinned. He was used to his boss's grouchy moods. Buck Campbell knew that was one reason Vern enjoyed ragging him so much. The sheriff kept threatening to fire him, but Vern did not seem worried.

Campbell shook his head, seeing that his comment had slid right off Vern's back, as usual. The boy was mighty sure of himself, and that meant a better man was liable to take him down someday . . . hard.

The sheriff was well aware that Vern had his eye on the top job. One of these days, Vern had said more than once, he was going to be running things around here. And he seemed to have the idea that one of the things he was going to be running was Hannah Campbell.

Vern was handsome enough, Buck Campbell supposed. He had curly brown hair and a quick grin, and he had a lot of the ladies in town charmed. Campbell had a feeling that Hannah was not among that number, though. That would probably just make Vern want her that much more.

"Ain't you got anything to do right now, Vern?" Campbell asked.

"I'm waiting for the stagecoach. That's part of a lawman's duties, isn't it—checking on all the newcomers?"

Campbell shrugged. Vern had a point. In a place that was growing as fast as Bonanza City, a lawman had to keep track of the comings and goings as best he could. He tried to keep the undesirables out of town, although with as many mines as there were in the area, it was a losing battle. Anywhere there was a lot of money floating around, there were going to be gamblers and whores and cutthroats.

Vern nudged him and pointed down the street. "There's the stage," he said. "But who the hell's that?"

Campbell frowned. It was not unusual for a stage to be so full that some of the passengers had to ride on top, but not in chains. And this coach definitely had a man chained on its roof.

As the coach came to a halt, the Campbell girls swarmed forward to greet Hannah. They were waiting when she swung the door open and stepped out, and they bunched around her in a flurry of hugs and squeals.

"Howdy, boys," Campbell greeted the driver and the guard. He jerked a thumb at the prisoner. "What've you got there?"

One of the passengers climbing down from the coach answered Campbell's question. "That's Sonora Pike, Sheriff," the tall, rawboned man said. "He's my prisoner, and I'd be obliged if you'd let me stash him in your jail."

Vern Simmons stared up at the man atop the stage. "Sonora Pike, the outlaw killer?"

"That's right, mister. What about it, Sheriff? Can you hold him?"

Campbell looked intently at the tall man, and then he asked, "You a lawman, a marshal maybe?"

The man shook his head. "Nope. Bounty hunter. Name's Rory Darson."

Campbell frowned and said nothing for a moment. Vern Simmons was more open in his reaction. "Bounty hunter, eh?" His contempt was plain in his voice. "I'm not sure your kind is welcome in our town, mister."

Rory glanced at him and took in the deputy's badge on his chest, but otherwise ignored him. He looked to Buck Campbell for an answer to his question.

The sheriff sighed. "We'll lock him up," he said heavily. "I ain't happy about having somebody like that in my jail, though."

"That's better than having Pike running around loose," Rory Darson pointed out.

"Reckon you're right. Well, get him down from there."

As Rory climbed onto the stage to unlock the chains holding Pike, Campbell swept his gaze over the other passengers getting off. He recognized Calhoun from a swing the drummer had made through the territory the year before. There was a preacher who did not take any baggage from the coach's boot, so he was probably traveling on. The other two passengers were the ones that Campbell could not get a handle on.

They looked like city folks, especially the man. The woman was a real beauty, Campbell had to admit. He had been happily married for twenty years and since the death of his wife had settled down to the life of a widower, but he could still appreciate a pretty gal. This newcomer with the dark blue eyes was that, sure enough. But there was something about her that struck a warning note in his instincts.

They were dressed a little too well to be a cardsharp and a soiled dove, Campbell decided, but he was going to keep his eye on them anyway.

Vern Simmons was waiting for his opportunity to welcome Hannah Campbell home, and as soon as the sisterly furor over her return had died down a little, he stepped forward and swept her into his arms. He kissed her soundly, holding her tightly in his embrace, but Hannah pulled back after a moment, looking uncomfortable and embarrassed.

"I declare, Vern Simmons, you are the most brazen man I've ever seen!" she scolded him. "I should slap your face."

Vern grinned cockily at her. "But you're not going to, are you?"

Hannah smiled. "No, I don't suppose I am."

Buck Campbell was frowning slightly at the exchange between his daughter and his deputy, and when he glanced up at the top of the stage, he saw that Rory Darson was watching them, too. He was a little surprised that some horsing around between two young people would distract a hard man like the bounty hunter.

Could it be that Rory Darson liked the looks of Hannah? Campbell grimaced and tried to shove that thought out of his head. Trouble like that was the last thing he needed, especially now when he was going to have a desperado like Sonora Pike in his lockup.

Rory Darson put his attention back on what he was doing. He did not think Pike would try to make a break right here in the middle of town with a sheriff and a deputy standing by, but there was no point in tempting him. When Rory had the chains unlocked, he dropped lithely from the top of the stage to the street and stepped back with his hand on his gun.

"All right, Pike," he said. "Climb down from there."

Stiffly, Pike stepped onto the box and then on down to the street. Buck Campbell drew his pistol and pointed. "Jail's down yonder," he told Pike. "Get moving."

With a sullen expression, the outlaw began walking toward the solidly built wooden structure that housed the sheriff's office and the lockup. Rory and Campbell stayed a little behind him, one on each flank.

Noticing the rough bandage on Pike's shoulder, Campbell asked the bounty hunter, "What happened there?"

"Bullet wound," Rory answered. "We threw some lead at each other when I caught up to him. It's not much, but I don't reckon it would hurt to have a doctor look at it."

Campbell nodded. He called out to one of the townspeople to tell Doc Madison to come down to the sheriff's office. The man hurried away.

The jail was typical of many that Rory had seen. The office was small and dark, with a battered desk and a few rough chairs. The cellblock was behind a thick log wall. As he and Buck Campbell ushered Pike into one of the cells, Rory grasped a bar and gave it a shake.

"Don't you worry, son," the sheriff told him. "I ain't had anybody break out of here yet, and I don't reckon Pike will, either."

Rory nodded. The sound of the door clanging shut behind Pike was a relief. He had not slept or even relaxed for at least twenty-four hours, and the strain was beginning to catch up to him.

He and the sheriff walked back into the office, leaving

the cellblock door open. As Campbell settled down into the chair behind his desk, Rory asked, "Do you have a telegraph here?"

The sheriff shook his head. "Nope. But I'll get a note off to the state capital right away to let them know that you've brought in Pike. They'll send some boys to pick him up."

"And bring the reward money."

"Yeah, and bring the reward money." Campbell looked intently at the tall bounty hunter. "Reckon that's all that matters to you, ain't it?"

"I never said that, Sheriff. But that is part of it. I won't deny it. Reckon I'm glad to have Pike where he can't hurt anybody else, too."

"Let's hope so." Campbell picked up a pen and pulled a piece of paper in front of him. "It'll take a few days to get everything squared away, maybe as long as a week. Hope you don't mind staying in town that long."

The prospect of spending a week in Bonanza City did not appeal much to Rory, but there was no way around it. He supposed he could leave a forwarding address with Campbell and have the sheriff send the reward to him, but he did not like to take chances with that much money. Besides, he had not decided where he intended to head from here.

"I'll stick around," he said.

The door opened, and a small man with a beard came into the office. He was carrying a black bag, and Rory knew he had to be the doctor. The man said, "They tell me you've got Sonora Pike locked up in here, Buck."

"They tell you right, Doc. He's back there in the cell with a bullet hole in his shoulder." Campbell put his palms on the desk and shoved himself to his feet. "Come on, I'll let you in to take a look at him."

Doc Madison cast a glance up at Rory as he went by. "You the man who put the bullet through his shoulder?" he asked.

Rory nodded. "I am."

"Why didn't you aim for his head?" the doctor snapped.

"I did." Rory grinned. That was not strictly true, but at

the time, he had not been too particular about where his shots landed. Not with Pike shooting back at him.

Rory leaned against the doorjamb while Madison examined Pike. Buck Campbell stood just outside the cell, his gun drawn and ready. The doctor removed the bandage, disinfected the wound, and covered it with a clean dressing. When he was done, he snapped his bag closed and came out of the cell, which Campbell locked behind him.

In the office, Madison said to Rory, "Looks like you did a fair job of patching him up, young man."

"A man in my line of work learns how to take care of bullet wounds."

"You could have been more careful about keeping it clean. Still, I didn't see any sign of festering."

As the doctor left, Rory turned back to the sheriff and asked, "Is there a good boardinghouse here in town where I could stay while I'm waiting for that reward money?"

"There's Ma Donohue's place. It's pretty clean, and she serves good meals. Or you could always get a room at the hotel."

Rory shook his head. "I'm afraid my wallet wouldn't stand up to renting a hotel room for a week."

"Well, I'll do what I can to get that reward through for you."

Rory thought he detected a slight tone of distaste in Campbell's voice, as if the sheriff wanted him out of Bonanza City as soon as possible. That did not surprise him, having dealt with lawmen all over the West. Most of them regarded bounty hunters as trouble.

A soft laugh on the boardwalk outside made Rory turn toward the door. It opened, and Hannah Campbell and Vern Simmons came in, arm in arm. The young deputy said, "I thought I'd better tell you that I'm going to help Hannah tote her bags home, Buck. You get that prisoner locked up all right?"

Campbell's shaggy red brows drew down. "Of course I did. Didn't notice you helping, though."

"Vern was helping me get my things off the stage, Pa," Hannah said.

"Well, I suppose that's all right."

Hannah looked at Rory and said, "The stage has already left, Mr. Darson. The driver had your horse taken down to the livery stable."

"Thanks for telling me," Rory replied. "Reckon I'd best go make arrangements for him to stay there a few days."

"Oh? You're staying on in Bonanza City?" There was a coolness in Hannah's voice.

Campbell answered his daughter's question. "Just until the reward money comes through. Right, Darson?"

Rory looked at Hannah for a long moment and then said slowly, "Yeah."

Vern Simmons put his arm around Hannah's shoulder and said, "Let's hope it comes soon."

Hannah stiffened slightly, and Rory saw something flare in her eyes as she pulled away from Vern. "In that case," she said, "I insist that you join us for dinner tonight, Mr. Darson."

"What?" The exclamation came from Campbell and Vern at the same time.

"My family and I like to make sure that newcomers feel welcome," Hannah went on. "Isn't that right, Pa?"

The sheriff made no reply, but only stared at her. Rory could see that Campbell and Vern were as surprised by the invitation as he was. Hannah had made it plain how she felt about bounty hunters, and now she was inviting him to her house.

If she could be contrary, so could he. Rory smiled at her and said, "Why, I'd sure be honored to accept your invitation, Miss Campbell. What time?"

"I think seven o'clock would be fine. We'll see you then, Mr. Darson." She glanced at her father. "Good-bye, Pa. Come on, Vern." She took the deputy's arm again and gently swung him toward the door.

When Hannah and Vern were gone, Rory turned to Buck Campbell and said, "What about it, Sheriff?"

Campbell took a deep breath. "An invite is an invite. You'll be welcome at my table tonight, Darson."

"I'd better find that boardinghouse and get spruced up, then." Rory left the office with a perverse grin on his face, listening to the sheriff muttering behind him.

*   *   *

Natalie Ingram was standing at the window of her room
on the hotel's second floor, watching the busy street below
her. She had removed her hat and undone the careful
arrangement of her hair, letting it flow darkly over her
shoulders. There was a slight smile on her full red lips,
and she murmured quiet words to herself as she concentrated her gaze on a wagon passing by in the dusty street.

"What's that you're saying, Natalie?" Stefan Kendrick
asked from behind her. He was unpacking her bags. His
own luggage was in his room across the hall. They had
taken separate quarters, as they usually did for propriety's
sake, but both of them knew where Kendrick would be
spending his nights.

Down in the street, one of the wagon's wheels suddenly
came off its axle, making the vehicle come to a grinding
halt. The load of supplies was dumped into the street as
the grizzled driver fell awkwardly off the box and began to
curse venomously.

Natalie's smile widened. "Nothing, Stefan," she said to
him, then continued in a whisper, "Nothing you would
understand."

The spell had worked beautifully. It was important for a
witch to practice her incantations, Natalie knew, to keep
her powers strong and effective. Some people might say
that the wagon wheel was simply worn and had broken in
a natural manner, but she knew better.

It was vital now that her powers be at their strongest.
She had a sacred mission to perform, and she would let
nothing stand in her way.

Kendrick came up behind her, having finished unpacking for her. His arms went around her, and his hands
found the thrust of her breasts. She let her weight sag into
him, closing her eyes as his lips grazed her neck through
her dark curtain of hair. Softly, she said, "It was quite a
long journey, Stefan."

"Are you tired, my dear?"

"A little."

She could feel his leer even though she could not see it.
"Then bed is the best place for you."

He began to unbutton her dress. She made no protest
as he undressed her. The hotel was one of the few two-
story buildings in Bonanza City, and none of the others
were located so that they had a view through the window,
so she did not worry about the curtain being open.

When she was nude, he turned her around and bent
slightly to kiss her breasts, lingering over the small, deep
red mark in the valley between them. He thought it was a
birthmark, but he was wrong about that, too.

It was the mark of Satan, Natalie thought as Kendrick
kissed it. Her witch's mark. Pride surged through her.

He urged her to the bed, lowering her to the mattress.
Natalie accepted whatever he did, compliant but not enthusiastic. As he moved over her and began to make love
to her, her mind cleared. She was a vessel for his lust,
nothing more.

If Kendrick knew she was distracted, he gave no sign of
it, taking his time with his pleasure, finally gasping out his
satisfaction. When he was done, he rolled from her, out of
breath.

A few moments later he raised himself on one elbow
and looked down at her. "We'd better talk about Winborn," he said.

Natalie sat up, not bothering to pull the sheet over her
nakedness. Nudity, after all, was the desired state for a
witch. She had read every book on the subject she could
find since that day when she had first experienced Satan's
presence. She had learned the rituals and the spells. She
knew that in some places there were whole covens of
believers who worshiped Lucifer and did his bidding here
on earth, but so far she had encountered none of them.
She was alone.

She shook her head, putting those thoughts away.
Kendrick was right, so far as he knew. They had come to
Bonanza City because of the wealthy mineowner named
Odell Winborn, whose success they had read about in
newspapers and magazines, and they needed to discuss
their plan of action.

It would probably be simple enough to get what they
wanted, Natalie knew. She and Kendrick had been part-

ners for several years now, and in that time, they had
fleeced over a dozen lonely, middle-aged rich men. Winborn would be one more mark to add to that score. With
her lush beauty and Kendrick's years of experience swin-
dling the wealthy, Winborn would not stand a chance.

Kendrick was talking about how they would set up their
supposedly chance meeting with Winborn, but he broke
off abruptly and said sharply, "Are you listening, Natalie?"

"Of course I am, Stefan," she insisted. "You were just
saying that Winborn drives his carriage from his office to
his home every evening at the same time."

"That's right. Pay attention, now."

Natalie's mind wandered, although she still appeared to
be listening raptly to Kendrick. If he knew the real reason
she had come to this part of the territory, he would be
shocked.

Just as Natalie had been shocked earlier in the day
when the quest that had taken years of her life had come
to a climax at a squalid little stagecoach station in the
middle of nowhere.

The man who was now called Sonora Pike had not
recognized her, but she had known him immediately. She
had betrayed no outward indication of it, but her heart
had broken at the sight of him, wounded and handcuffed
and then chained to the top of the coach.

That bounty hunter, the one called Rory Darson, would
pay for treating her brother that way.

She had been only a child when her brother had ridden
away from the family farm for the last time, but even
though sixteen years had passed, the memories were still
painfully vivid. To the twelve-year-old Natalie, he was the
center of her life, the adored older brother who had
always looked out for her and given her the love that their
parents and the other children did not.

For a while he had written to her, but then the letters
stopped coming. Word trickled back to Missouri that he
had gone bad and become an outlaw. He had taken to
calling himself Sonora Pike. Natalie had always told herself that he had changed his name so that he would not
bring shame on the family, but she knew deep down that

the name he had taken was a lot more fitting for a desperado than his real name, Arthur Ingram. If he wanted to be
Sonora Pike, that was fine with her.

When she was old enough, she had left home, too, and
headed west to find him. While he was gone, the devotion
to witchcraft had come to her, and the two things had
somehow gotten tied together in her brain. Finding her
brother was to be the culmination of her bargain with the
devil, and when Kendrick had suggested that they head
for Bonanza City, Natalie knew that a dark hand was really
behind the flow of events. She knew that Sonora Pike had
been reported in that vicinity, and it seemed that her long
search was about to come to an end.

And now . . . now it had come to pass.

She had found her brother, but he was locked up in the
local jail. She had seen the bounty hunter and the sheriff
taking him there, and she knew that he would be held for
other authorities. Eventually, he would be tried, con-
victed, and hung.

But not if there was anything she could do about it. She
had not spent years searching for Sonora Pike, only to
have him taken away from her once she had found him.
Somehow, she vowed, she would set him free.

And with all the powers of evil to aid her, she would
have her revenge on the man who had wounded and
captured her brother.

Before he died, Rory Darson would know hell on earth.

Chapter Four

Sonora Pike called from the cellblock, "Hey, Deputy, when do you plan on feedin' me?"

Vern Simmons had his booted feet on the desk as he leaned back in the sheriff's chair. It was early evening, and the lamp on the desk was lit. Not much light got into the office through the narrow windows during the day, and once the sun was down the shadows gathered quickly.

"Keep your shirt on, Pike," Vern replied without turning around. He was struggling with the string tie around his neck. A tie was a damned foolish invention, as far as he was concerned, but he wanted to look good tonight. He had even put on a clean shirt. He went on, "The girl from the café will be here in a little bit with your supper."

"Hope she hurries," Pike grumbled. "That no-good bounty hunter don't believe in feedin' a man."

"That so?" Vern asked, eager to hear anything bad about Rory Darson. He had disliked the man on sight, over and above the fact that he was a bounty hunter. Maybe it had something to do with the way Rory Darson looked at Hannah.

Vern frowned at the thought. He would soon put a stop to that. Not that there was anything there to stop, he added hastily to himself.

He had hardly been able to believe his ears when Hannah invited the man to dinner. The thought of a bloody-handed man-hunter sitting down to dine with the Campbells was infuriating. But Vern would be there to make sure there was no trouble. He had invited himself, and Hannah had not told him not to come.

He heard the clicking of heels on the boardwalk outside, and then the door swung open. Ellen Harwood stepped into the office, carrying a tray of food in one hand with practiced ease. A smile lit up her broad face when she saw Vern sitting at the desk.

"Hello, Vern," she said warmly. "I've got the supper for your prisoner."

"Howdy," the deputy grunted, swinging his feet off the desk and standing up. He crossed the room and put his hands out for the tray. "Reckon I'd better take that."

"Sure, Vern." Ellen handed over the tray, her fingers brushing against Vern's. He turned and started toward the cellblock.

Ellen Harwood was a young woman of twenty-three, the same age as Hannah Campbell. She owned the nearby café and had a contract with the county to feed whatever prisoners were being held in the jail. She sometimes brought meals for the sheriff and the deputy, as well, but Vern had stopped by her place earlier and told her to prepare only one tray tonight.

Like Hannah, Ellen also wore her hair in braids wrapped around her head, but hers were blond. Her figure was sturdy, her bosom impressive. It did not seem to impress Vern Simmons, however. In fact, he seldom had a second glance for Ellen.

Having heard a female voice, Pike leaned forward in his cell, pressing his face against the bars. As Vern appeared in the door to the cellblock, Pike said, "You got a woman out there, Deputy?"

"I told you, the girl from the café brought your supper," Vern replied.

"Well, trot her back here for me, why don't you?" An ugly grin stretched across Pike's face. "Maybe I could nibble on her for dessert, huh?"

"Shut your mouth and back off from those bars," Vern snapped.

Behind him, Ellen stepped into the doorway. She had

heard Vern's responses but not Pike's comments. "Is everything all right, Vern?" she asked.

Pike's eyes locked on her, his gaze moving slowly, brazenly, over her body. He took in her breasts and the swell of her hips, and his tongue licked over his dry lips. "A little hefty," he said, "but I reckon she'll do. Man as lonely as I been ain't too picky."

Vern's hand fell to the butt of his gun. "I told you to shut up," he growled. "Now if you want this food, back off." Over his shoulder, he snapped, "Ellen, you get back in the office."

Ellen flushed in embarrassment at Pike's comments, but her eyes seemed to glow when Vern spoke up in her defense. "Yes, Vern," she said quietly, stepping back so that Pike could no longer see her. She could still see the deputy, though, as he passed the tray to Pike through the slot in the bars. Then he stalked back into the office, shaking his head.

"Figured you'd have more sense than to pull something like that," he said. "No point in stirring up a prisoner."

"Why, Vern, I never thought about getting him stirred up. You think I did?"

"You're a woman, aren't you?"

"Some people think so." Ellen's tone was a little stiff. She went to the door and paused before going out. "Are you having dinner at Hannah's tonight?"

"I thought I would, as soon as Luke Warner gets here to keep an eye on Pike." Luke was a young man who had been a bust as a miner, but he made a good part-time deputy and jailer for Buck Campbell. "That bounty hunter's going to be there, so I thought I'd better be, too."

"Well . . . have a good time."

Vern frowned at the desk when Ellen was gone. He had seen her and talked to her nearly every day for months, but there were times when she surely did act a mite strange. It was more than he could figure out, but he knew one thing—he was not going to waste a lot of time worrying over it. Not when he had more important things to worry about.

Like Hannah and that bounty hunter.

*   *   *

The boardinghouse lived up to Buck Campbell's recommendation, Rory discovered. It was clean, and the widow lady who ran it was pleasant enough. His room was narrow, but it had a window, and the bed felt mighty good when he sat down on it to test it. He had gotten his saddlebags and his pack from the livery stable when he had paid the hostler for taking care of the horse. That had depleted his funds even more, leaving him just enough to pay for his room. It was a good thing he had been invited to dinner tonight. He would have to speak to the sheriff tomorrow about advancing him some money on the reward that was on the way.

There was a pump behind the boardinghouse, and in the fading light Rory washed up and scraped the stubble off his face. He dug out a shirt from his pack that was a little wrinkled but clean and put it on. As he got ready to head to the Campbell house, his thoughts kept straying back to Hannah.

She was a woman who did not hesitate to speak her mind. The conversation on the stage had proved that. She had probably asked him to supper just out of sheer cussedness, he decided—or maybe she thought it would give her a good opportunity to chew on him some more about the way he treated his prisoners.

But she might just have felt sorry for him after hearing about how his family had died. As he dusted off his hat and then settled it on his head, it occurred to him that he might be feeling a little too uncharitable toward Hannah. She might just want to make sure a stranger had a good meal on his first night in town.

He left the boardinghouse after Ma Donohue told him where the sheriff lived. The stroll down the street took him through Bonanza City as night was falling. Even now the street was full of men and horses and wagons. The stores were open and doing good business, and all of the saloons were brightly lit. Music and laughter floated out of them, and the sound was a powerful temptation. But Rory walked on, past the twin lures of drink and women, toward the Campbell house. There would be time for the other *after* supper.

The sheriff and his family lived in a good-sized frame structure with a covered porch built along the front. There were a couple of small pine trees in the front yard. The light coming from inside was warm and yellow and inviting as Rory stepped up onto the porch and knocked on the door.

It was opened a moment later by Buck Campbell. He had taken off his hat and his revolver, and in his hand was an old briarwood pipe. "Come on in, Darson," he said, stepping back from the door. There was not much warmth in his voice, but Rory could not detect any hostility, either.

As he stepped inside, Rory's gaze took in the room, which was large and high ceilinged. A long table covered with a linen cloth took up the rear of the room. In the front corner was a fireplace, with several armchairs drawn up before it. A low divan ran along the wall, and a thick rug lay in the center of the floor. Through an open door, Rory could see part of the kitchen, which was filled at the moment by redheaded Campbell girls. Hannah was at the stove, her face flushed prettily by the heat.

Standing in the center of the room was the young deputy, Vern Simmons, his figure stiff with belligerence. He did not look happy to see Rory.

"Have a seat," Campbell said to Rory. "Let me have your hat." He took the hat and hung it on a peg near the door while Rory walked slowly over to Vern.

"Howdy," Rory said. "I figured you'd be over at the jail keeping an eye on Pike."

"He's in good hands," Vern replied tightly.

"My jailer's over there," Campbell put in. "He's a good lad, Darson. You don't have to worry. And I'll be going over later to relieve him."

Rory nodded. "Pike's slippery. You can't blame a man for worrying about him."

"He won't get away before you get your reward," Vern said.

Rory felt his nerves growing taut. The deputy's contempt grated on him, especially here where Hannah could overhear. There was no good reason for her presence to affect his behavior, but he could not deny that he wanted her to see that she had misjudged him. He would not accomplish that by starting a ruckus in her house.

With an effort, he put a smile on his face and willed his muscles to relax. "That's mighty good to hear," he said softly.

Hannah came out of the kitchen then, wiping her hands on a cloth. "Good evening, Mr. Darson," she said. "I'm glad you could come."

"Thanks again for inviting me."

"I want you to meet my sisters." She gestured for them to come out of the kitchen. Each of the girls carried a platter of food and placed it on the table as Hannah performed the introductions. "This is Bess, Dinah, Melanie, and Emily. Girls, this is Mr. Rory Darson."

Rory nodded at them and said as gallantly as possible, "Ladies, I'm right honored to meet you."

They all smiled and murmured shy greetings, except for the youngest, Emily, whom Rory judged to be about five or six years old. She stared up at him with wide eyes, obviously impressed. When she had put down the plate of biscuits she was carrying, she came over to him, craned her neck, and said, "You're the tallest feller I ever saw."

Rory grinned down at her. "Reckon I must've got stretched somewhere."

Hannah put her hand on Emily's shoulder and gently guided her back to the table. "Why don't we all sit down?" she said.

Buck Campbell took his place at the head of the table and motioned for Rory to sit at his left. Emily scurried over to take the chair next to him, and Rory knew that he had made one conquest tonight. The little girl smiled broadly when he glanced down at her. Hannah sat at her father's right, directly across the table from Rory, while Vern Simmons claimed the seat next to her. He held Hannah's chair for her, and there was a possessiveness about the way he performed the act that rankled Rory.

Once the other girls had taken their places, Buck Campbell quieted their chatter with a look and then said grace. As Rory bowed his head, he felt someone watching him, and through slitted eyes he saw that it was Hannah. He closed his eyes, not wanting to embarrass her.

The dinner was one of the best he had ever had. Hannah had fried a couple of chickens, and the younger girls had prepared peas and potatoes and beans. The light, fluffy biscuits were a far cry from the ones he cooked for himself on the trail. With butter and honey, Rory could have made a meal on them alone. The table was surrounded by talk and laughter and all the warmth of family. As he sat there and ate, Rory felt a pang deep inside his belly, something almost like pain.

He was enjoying himself.

It had been so long since he had experienced anything like this. He usually took his meals alone, unless he had a prisoner with him. Casting his memory back over the years, he realized that this was the first time he had eaten a meal in good company since his own family had been killed. The evening would have been perfect if it had not been for Vern Simmons sitting across the table and giving him the evil eye.

"Tell me, Mr. Darson," Hannah asked, "what do you think of Bonanza City?"

"Seems like a nice enough place," Rory answered slowly. "It's cleaner than some of the mining towns I've seen."

"Been around a lot, have you?" Campbell said before taking a bite of chicken.

"More than enough."

Emily, her voice enthusiastic, said, "I'll bet you've been everywhere, Mr. Darson!"

Rory grinned down at her as Hannah said, "Emily! Don't bother Mr. Darson."

"No bother," Rory said. Looking at Emily, he went on, "Reckon you're just about right, little miss. There's bound to be a few spots I've missed, but I've pretty well been from one end of the West to the other."

"I don't suppose most folks want a bounty hunter in their parts for very long," Vern put in. "That's probably why Mr. Darson has traveled so much, Emily."

Hannah shot a sharp glance at Vern, and Campbell frowned at his deputy's sarcastic words. Rory was a guest in their home, after all.

Mentally, Rory shook off the surge of anger he felt. He did not want any trouble tonight. He said to Emily, "Vern might be right, but that just gives me an excuse to move on when the time comes."

"You've never felt like settling down?" Hannah asked.

"Never saw any need to," Rory answered honestly. "There's always other places to go, other things to see."

"Other men to hunt down," Vern said.

Rory took a deep breath and stared across the table at him for a long moment and then said quietly, "Reckon so."

A part of him wanted to lunge across the table and plant his fist right in the middle of Vern's smirk. For two cents, he thought, he would do just that. He did not know why he was worried about what Hannah and the other Campbells thought of him. The evening had been pleasant enough, for the most part, but it was not going to lead anywhere. When the reward money for Pike came through, Rory would collect it, leave Bonanza City, and probably never see any of these people again. That thought pained him some, but that was the way it had to be.

Hannah was glaring angrily at Vern, and for some reason that made Rory feel better. Maybe he had won her over a bit, had shown her that he was not some sort of monster just because he happened to be a bounty hunter.

Buck Campbell changed the subject, talking about the mines in the area, relating how a miner's excited cry of "It's a bonanza!" had given the town its name. As the settlement had grown, there had been need of a lawman, and Campbell had been hired away from a similar position in a town on the other side of the Sangre de Cristos. The family had quickly settled in. Campbell concluded by saying, "I reckon we'll stay here as long as they'll have us. It's a good place to live, and I'm getting on toward the time when I'll be wanting to take off this star and hang up my guns."

"Well, when that time comes, you won't have to worry

about a thing, Buck," Vern said smoothly. "The county will be in good hands." He looked directly at Rory and went on, "I'll make sure the undesirable elements don't come in and take over."

Rory folded his napkin, put it on the table, and pushed back his chair. "That was a mighty fine meal, ladies," he said, his anger under control but just barely. "I sure do appreciate it. I'd better be moving on now."

"But we've got deep-dish apple pie for dessert!" Emily exclaimed.

Rory reached out and patted her shoulder. "I'm plumb full, Miss Emily, but thank you, anyway. Some other time, maybe."

Campbell stood up. "Here, now, we haven't had brandy and cigars yet, Darson. Bonanza City's a civilized town. Wouldn't want you thinking otherwise."

"Don't worry, Sheriff. I don't."

Vern stood up as well. He grinned and said, "You go right ahead, Darson. I'm sure you've got important things to do."

Rory glanced around the table, saw the tenseness on the faces of the girls, and regretted the way things had turned out. He could see now that Vern Simmons was not going to let it rest, so he decided the best thing would be for him to leave.

He took his hat from the peg and settled it on his head, aware that Vern had come around the table and was moving along behind him. He wondered what else the arrogant young pup wanted.

"See you tomorrow, Sheriff," Rory said as he opened the door and stepped out onto the porch. He looked back into the warmth and met Hannah's eyes. "So long, Miss Hannah," he added.

Vern sidled into the doorway, coming between Rory and Hannah. In a low voice, he said, "Don't you come back here, Darson."

Rory met his stare. "Why not, Deputy?"

"Because this is a decent home. It's no place for bounty-hunting trash like you. You just stay away from the Campbells."

Rory's chest was tight with anger. "Especially Hannah, I reckon."

"Especially Hannah."

Rory started to turn away, wanting nothing now except to get away from here before the rein on his temper slipped. He had just stepped from the porch onto the ground when Vern, following, reached out and grabbed his shoulder, pulling him half around.

"I'm not through with you yet," he snapped.

"Damn right," Rory growled, his hard-won control finally evaporating. His right fist lashed out, driving hard into Vern's belly.

Vern bent over and took a step backward, air whooshing from his lungs. With a wild look in his eyes, he grated, "You bastard!" and launched himself forward.

He crashed into Rory, and both men staggered back. Rory's feet slipped on loose stones and he fell, taking Vern with him.

They landed hard, rolling apart and coming up on their feet at the same moment. Vern swung wildly at Rory's head. Rory ducked the punch easily and stepped inside, pounding Vern's middle with short, hard blows as rage gripped him. The deputy had been prodding him all night, ruining a perfectly good meal, and now by God he was going to get what he had been asking for!

Buck Campbell ran onto the porch with Hannah close behind him. She let out a cry of alarm. "Stop them, Pa!" she pleaded. The other girls crowded onto the porch behind her, their faces showing a mixture of horror and fascination.

"Here, now, you two!" Campbell shouted at the two brawling figures. "Stop that! Stop that fightin'!"

So far it had not been much of a fight. Vern Simmons had had his share of barroom fracases, both before and after becoming a deputy, but he was no match for a man like Rory, whose life had often depended on his fists. Rory battered him until Vern, backing away, bumped into one of the pines. With the tree trunk holding the deputy up, Rory swung a right and then a left, jerking Vern's head back and forth. Vern started to sag.

Rory caught the deputy's shirt with his left hand and held him up, cocking his right fist for another blow. But before he could throw the punch, hard fingers fastened on his wrist and an arm looped around his neck. Awkwardly, Buck Campbell pulled the taller man away from Vern.

The deputy took a couple of steps and then pitched forward on his face, lying limply on the ground. Rory, jerking out of Campbell's grasp, stared down at Vern. Blood pounded in his head, but he had his rage under control again now.

In a low voice, Campbell said, "You'd better get out of here, Darson. Vern's been asking for it all night, so I ain't going to press any charges against you, but I warn you, I won't stand for any more brawlin'! Not in my town. And certainly not in front of my family."

Rory drew a deep breath. "I understand, Sheriff. Your boy here shouldn't be hurt too bad."

"Just banged up, from the looks of it. Now go on, son."

Rory bent to pick up his hat, which had come off during the brief melee. As he did so, Hannah rushed past him, dropping to her knees beside Vern. Campbell stooped and rolled the deputy over, and Hannah lifted his head and cradled it in her lap.

Rory's mouth twitched grimly. It appeared that Hannah returned Vern's affection, after all. He had started to think that maybe the young man was forcing his attentions on her, but it did not look that way now. Lines of concern were etched on Hannah's face as she wiped away a trickle of blood oozing from the corner of Vern's mouth.

Sensing that the other girls were staring at him, Rory turned toward the porch and said, "I'm right sorry I've ruined the evening, ladies. It was a very pleasant dinner."

Bess, Dinah, and Melanie all glared at him, obviously upset at what he had done to Vern Simmons. Hannah and her father were angry with him, too. Emily, he thought wryly, was the only one who was not upset with him.

"Good night, Mr. Darson," the little girl called. "You'll come back and see us, won't you?"

"We'll see about that, Miss Emily." Rory turned and walked away from the Campbell house. He heard Vern moan, and his back burned where their eyes watched him go.

Earlier that evening, Natalie Ingram and Stefan Kendrick had put their plan into motion.

Natalie had waited just inside the door of the hotel until she had seen the black carriage pulled by two horses coming down the street toward her. The carriage was plainly appointed but obviously well made and expensive. On the seat was a middle-aged man in a dark suit and hat, and Natalie could see his thick sideburns and full mustache in the fading light. She knew that he had to be Odell Winborn.

She glanced at Kendrick, who was seated several feet away in an armchair, pretending to read a copy of the *Bonanza City Chronicle*. He nodded slightly, just enough for her to see.

Natalie took a deep breath and stepped out onto the boardwalk, moving quickly into the street. She seemed not to see the oncoming horses and carriage as she strolled in front of them.

Winborn let out a cry of alarm and hauled back on the reins when he saw the dark-haired young woman. Natalie's head jerked up, and she screamed as the team bore down on her. She took a quick step backward, losing her balance and throwing up her hands as she fell out of the way of the animals. Winborn hauled the team to a halt and then leaped down from the carriage.

"My word, are you all right, madam?" he asked anxiously as he bent to take Natalie's arm.

She looked up at him, her face pale, and a shudder went through her body. "I . . . I believe I am uninjured, sir," she gasped. "I am so sorry—"

"Nonsense," Winborn said. "My fault, all my fault. Here, let me assist you to your feet."

As Natalie was getting up, with Winborn's hand on her arm, Kendrick rushed from the porch of the hotel. "My God, Natalie!" he exclaimed. "Are you all right? What happened here?"

"I'm perfectly fine, Stefan," she assured him. "It was my own foolish fault. I was so engrossed with this quaint little town that I walked right out in front of this gentleman's carriage." She brushed the dirt from her dress, making sure to arch her back slightly so as to thrust her breasts out.

Winborn watched her for a moment and then tore his eyes away and turned to Kendrick. "My sincerest apologies, sir," he said. "I should have been watching where I was going. If I had seen your wife earlier, none of this would have happened."

Natalie laughed, her fright apparently over. The laugh was low and throaty, designed to strike a chord in any male who heard it. "Goodness, sir, I'm Stefan's cousin, not his wife."

"I value you as highly as if you were my wife," Kendrick said, touching her shoulder solicitously. "Are you sure you're all right?"

"I'm certain." She turned to the mineowner. "Now I don't want you concerning yourself over this, Mr. . . . ?"

"Winborn," he supplied. "Odell Winborn, at your service, ma'am."

Kendrick extended his hand. "Stefan Kendrick, sir," he said as they shook. "And this is my cousin, Natalie Ingram."

Winborn touched the brim of his soft felt hat. "It is an honor to meet you, Miss Ingram. I am only sorry that it had to be under such unpleasant circumstances."

"No harm done," Natalie said sweetly. "What lady could be upset about meeting a perfectly charming gentleman, no matter what the circumstances?"

Winborn flushed with embarrassment and pleasure as Natalie smiled at him, suppressing the contempt she felt for him. Men were so easy to manipulate. She had left her hair loose, a rather daring style for a lady to wear in public, and she knew the tight silk dress showed off her figure to its best advantage. A man like Winborn would be easily overwhelmed by her beauty. At least that was what she and Kendrick were counting on.

"You must allow me to do something to make up for the inconvenience I've caused you," Winborn was saying.

"There's no need," Natalie replied. "Stefan and I were just about to have dinner—"

"Then you shall have it with me," Winborn cut in, taking the bait at the first opportunity. "I insist. They know me down at the restaurant and know that I won't settle for anything less than the best. Please, both of you join me."

Natalie looked to Kendrick to make the decision. He smiled and said, "Well, if you insist, Mr. Winborn, we'll be glad to join you. To tell the truth, we're new in your community, and it will be an honor to have dinner with one of Bonanza City's leading citizens."

"You know of me?" Winborn asked.

The smile on Natalie's face never faltered, although the glance she shot toward Kendrick was like icy daggers. He had said too much, as he often did. Quickly, she said, "Why, anyone could tell merely by looking at you, Mr. Winborn, that you would be a leading citizen in any town!"

Again he smiled in pleasure, and she knew she had covered Kendrick's slip.

She linked arms with Kendrick, and they strolled down the boardwalk toward the café as Winborn climbed back into his carriage and flicked the reins to urge the team into motion. Natalie leaned her head close to Kendrick as they walked, and she whispered, "Be careful, Stefan. The man is no fool."

Kendrick smiled. "Any man who looks too long at you turns into a fool, my dear."

Winborn had been telling the truth. The owners of the restaurant made a fuss over him, escorting him and his guests to the best table and promising them the finest meal the cook could prepare.

The dinner went well. Natalie could tell that Winborn was taken with her, charmed by her beauty and grace. She knew from the articles she had read about Kendrick that the mineowner had never been married. His work was his passion. Once a hard-rock miner himself, it had been years since he had swung a pick, but he still spent many long, lonely hours working to make his mine pay off. He was a perfect target.

And he was not a bad-looking man, Natalie decided. His jaw was strong and firm, and there was only a touch of gray in his sandy hair. It was not required that the victims of their swindles be attractive, but it always helped Natalie make the charade more convincing.

At the right time, she asked sweetly, "And what do you do for a living, Mr. Winborn?"

"Why, I own the Vista mine," Winborn replied. "You might have heard of it."

"Yes, indeed," Kendrick said. "That's been quite a good claim, I hear."

Winborn shrugged. "The men and I have worked hard to make it so. It's not along the same lines as the Bonanza or the Exchequer, but it's a good producer. You're familiar with mining, Mr. Kendrick?"

Natalie laughed. "Familiar? Stefan? Mr. Winborn, my cousin is a mining engineer. He's worked at some of the best mines in the West."

"Now, Natalie, you mustn't boast about me," Kendrick scolded with a smile. "Next to a man like Mr. Winborn here, I'm probably just a rank amateur."

"Oh, no, I'd be very interested to hear some of your theories, sir," Winborn said as he leaned forward. Natalie could tell from the glance he shot toward her that he was trying to impress her by being polite to Kendrick.

That was fine, just fine.

Her mind wandered as Kendrick and Winborn began talking about the mining industry. Kendrick was no engineer, but from his cursory study of current mining techniques, he was able to ask enough questions to sound as though he knew what he was talking about. Most of the conversation went over Natalie's head. She concentrated instead on her steak and the surprisingly good wine, making sure that she smiled at Winborn every time he glanced in her direction. She saw that his eyes were often drawn to her breasts, and she knew that he was being lured into her scheme.

When the meal was over, Winborn gave Kendrick a fat

cigar, which the tall man lit and puffed upon gratefully. "This was certainly a fine evening, Mr. Winborn," he said.

"Yes, indeed," Natalie echoed. "We do appreciate it, Mr. Winborn."

Winborn drained the last of his wine and grinned at her. "Please, my dear, call me Odell."

"Well . . . all right, Odell. But only if you'll call me Natalie."

"And I'm Stefan," Kendrick added. The feeling of friendship around the table was strong, a tribute to the acting skills of two of the people seated there.

"Stefan, I'd like for you to come out to the Vista with me tomorrow," Winborn said. "That is, if you have the time."

"This is a pleasure trip for us, Odell. We've nothing but time," Kendrick replied. "I'd be glad to look over your operation."

"Perhaps you could give me some suggestions for improving it. I don't want to ruin your vacation—"

"Nonsense," Kendrick said, waving the cigar expansively. "It would be a pleasure for me."

"You're welcome to come along, too, of course, Miss Natalie," Winborn said, turning to her.

"Just Natalie, remember?" She smiled as she shook her head. "Unlike my cousin, I don't have a great deal of interest in holes in the ground, Odell."

"Then what about dinner again tomorrow night?" The desire in Winborn's voice was so plain to Natalie that it was all she could do not to laugh in his face.

"That would be very nice," she murmured, holding his gaze, putting all sorts of hints and promises in the quiet, simple words.

After Winborn paid for the meal, the three of them paused on the boardwalk outside the restaurant. Night had fallen, and although there was a great deal of raucous noise coming from the saloons at the other end of town, this part of the street was quiet. Winborn shook hands with Kendrick and then took Natalie's hand. His fingers were warm, his palm slightly damp. Natalie showed no sign of the revulsion she felt.

"Until tomorrow night, then, Natalie," he said.

"Yes," she breathed. "Until tomorrow . . ."

As they watched him drive away in the carriage, Kendrick said quietly, "I think it went very well, don't you?"

"He's pitiful," Natalie said, after glancing around to make sure that no one was nearby to overhear her words. "This should be very easy, Stefan."

"Let's hope so." He took her arm and started back toward the hotel.

They got the keys to both of their rooms from the desk clerk, keeping up the masquerade of being cousins. Kendrick bid her good night, and she went upstairs by herself while he settled down in one of the lobby arm-chairs to finish his cigar and glance again at the newspaper. As she let herself into her room, she knew that he would be joining her in a few minutes. He would want her again tonight, would want to relax after the strain of the evening.

Sure enough, the door opened ten minutes later and Kendrick slipped inside. Natalie had turned the lamp on the bureau down low before she began undressing, and now a soft, warm light filled the room as she turned toward Kendrick.

She wore dark stockings and a black corset, the garments providing a sensuous contrast with her pale skin. As she moved into Kendrick's arms, his right hand cupped her left breast. He needed this—and right now, so did she.

Kendrick fell asleep afterwards, as he usually did. Tonight, Natalie had intended that he doze off quickly, so she had been more enthusiastic than usual. He was snoring deeply as she slipped out of the rumpled bed.

Nude, she padded to the window and pushed back the curtain so that moonlight would spill through and cast a square of illumination on the floor. Opening the top drawer of the bureau, she took out several candles and a piece of chalk.

Quickly, she drew a simple, five-pointed design on the floor, placing a candle at each of the points. When she had

them lit, she blew out the lamp, leaving the room in
shadow for the most part. The candles gave off little light,
just enough for the pentagram to be seen.

Sinking to her knees next to the mystic drawing, Natalie
threw her head back and closed her eyes. Her lips began
to move as she whispered words that had never before
been heard in Bonanza City, words that had their origin
far back in time. As she spoke the words of the spells, her
hands came up and caressed herself, the fingertips moving
lingeringly over breasts and thighs. Lost in the ritual, she
swayed slightly from side to side as the spirits revealed
their message to her.

All the portents were right, she realized as she opened
her eyes and slumped to the floor, drained by the experience she had just had. As she caught her breath, she knew
that the time had come. She dressed quickly and quietly,
not wanting to disturb Kendrick. She glanced at his sleeping form and smiled grimly. She had exhausted him; he
would not awaken until long after she had returned from
her mission.

The lobby was deserted when she went downstairs. The
clerk was probably asleep on the cot in the little room
behind the desk. That was good. She did not want any
witnesses to her actions.

Slipping out of the hotel, she turned down the boardwalk, heading toward the Bonanza City jail.

Chapter Five

Bonanza City was relatively peaceful as Buck Campbell made his nightly rounds. There was the usual uproar in the saloons as miners and cowhands blew off steam, but nothing was going on that required his attention. The saloons had their own bouncers to handle all but the worst trouble. The other business establishments along the street were darkened and locked.

Campbell finished his turn around the town and returned to the jail. When he rapped on the thick wooden door, Luke Warner called from inside, "Who is it?"

"It's me, Luke," the sheriff replied.

The young jailer unlocked the door and swung it open. He was tall and gangling and had never really been suited to being a miner, which was one good reason that he was now a part-time deputy.

"Any problems?" Campbell asked as he took off his hat and started to pour a cup of coffee.

"Nope, not a one. Pike's asleep." Luke's hand was on the butt of his gun, and he was clearly nervous. "I surely will be glad when them boys from the state capital pick him up. I don't like havin' a man like him in our jail."

"He's just a man," Campbell said, sitting down behind the desk. "Worse than most, but still a man."

"Reckon so, but some of them stories I've heard . . ." Luke swallowed. "You want me to stay around, Sheriff, to keep you company?"

"No, you go on home and get some sleep, Luke. I'm going to need you to relieve me in eight hours or so."

"What happened to Vern?"

Campbell grimaced. "He won't be in tonight. Never you mind why, all right?" The sheriff snorted at the memory of how Vern had looked, bloody and battered and not worthy of the name lawman at the moment.

"Sure, Sheriff. I'll be back 'fore dawn. You positive you'll be all right?"

"Told you I would be, didn't I? Now get your scrawny carcass on out of here."

Luke nodded, grinned weakly, and left. Buck Campbell heaved himself up out of the chair, went to the door, and relocked it.

As he settled himself down behind the desk again, Campbell opened one of the drawers and took out a book. He opened it, found his place from earlier in the day, and resumed reading the dime-novel exploits of Deadwood Dick. It was a particularly exciting story about the horrible depredations of the Washburn gang, and Campbell was soon absorbed in it. He did not forget about the real-life outlaw in the cellblock behind him, but at least he was able for a few moments to ease the strain he felt.

Time passed, and Campbell got up once to refill his coffee cup. A little after nine-thirty, when Deadwood Dick was just about to close in on the leader of the gang, a soft knock came on the door.

Campbell glanced up, surprised that he had a visitor this late. The knock had sounded like a woman's, and he supposed it could be Hannah, bringing him another piece of that apple pie. With that hope in mind, he went to the door and called, "Who's there?"

An unfamiliar female voice answered, "Please, Sheriff, I need to talk to you."

There was a touch of desperation in the woman's tone. The shutters were closed and fastened over the windows, so Campbell was prevented from looking out to see who was on the boardwalk. There was a small opening in the door itself, and he swung back the piece of wood covering it.

When he put his eye to the peephole, he saw a very
attractive woman with dark hair standing just outside the
door, an agitated expression on her lovely face. Campbell
recognized her as the woman who had come in on the
same stagecoach as Hannah that afternoon.

She seemed to be alone, and she certainly did not look
like any kind of threat. Campbell grunted, "Wait a minute," and dug out his key.

When he had the door open, she stepped quickly into
the office, casting a glance back over her shoulder. "Thank
God you are here, Sheriff," she said breathlessly.

"Here now, just settle down. What's the trouble, ma'am?
What can I do for you?"

"There's a prowler down at the hotel, Sheriff. Please,
can you come down there and arrest him?"

"A prowler? You sure, ma'am?" Such occurrences were
rare in Bonanza City, but Campbell supposed somebody
could be sneaking around the hotel looking for something
to steal.

"I'm certain. He came to my room and rattled the
doorknob. I was terrified."

"But the door was locked?"

"Of course. And when he couldn't get into my room, I
heard him creeping on down the hall. I'm sure he intends
to murder someone, Sheriff. I've heard that life is so
cheap here in the West."

Her voice was shaking nervously, and while Campbell
did not doubt her sincerity, he was starting to question
whether or not her claims were accurate. "Did you tell
Barney at the desk about what happened?"

"I . . . I summoned up my courage and went downstairs
to report the incident, but I couldn't find the clerk anywhere." The woman paused, a look of horror slowly growing on her face. "You don't suppose the prowler had
already killed him before I got to the lobby, do you?"

"Not likely," Campbell answered dryly. "Barney was
probably just catching a nap in the back room." He looked
thoughtful as he went on, "Were you asleep when this
fellow tried to get into your room, ma'am?"

"Well, yes, I was, but I woke up immediately."

Campbell nodded, beginning to understand what had likely happened. This young lady, obviously city-bred and a little nervous at being in a frontier town, had dreamt that someone was trying to break into her room, and upon awakening, she had mistaken the nightmare for reality. At least he hoped that was what had happened. With Sonora Pike in his jail, he could not leave to investigate something that had probably never happened.

"What you need right now, ma'am," he said, "is a cup of coffee. Settle those nerves of yours right down."

"I am not nervous, Sheriff," she insisted. "I know what I heard."

"I'm sure you do, ma'am." Another possibility occurred to him, and he continued, "But I reckon there's plenty of reasonable explanations for what went on. Somebody could've mistook your room for theirs, and they didn't realize they'd made a mistake until they tried the door and found it locked. As I recollect, the halls in the hotel ain't too brightly lit, and if somebody had, ah, overindulged at the saloon, it'd be easy to make a mistake like that."

His soothing, confident tone seemed to get through to the woman. She said tentatively, "I suppose that could have been what happened."

"Of course it could. Now let me get that coffee for you."

Campbell found a clean cup and poured the strong black brew. The woman stood beside the desk and sipped the coffee for a moment. Then she said, "I'm sorry I got all upset and came running down here, Sheriff. Now that I've thought about it, I'm sure your explanation was correct."

"That's just fine, ma'am. I don't reckon you've got a thing to worry about down there in the hotel. Nobody's going to bother you. This town's a little wild and woolly yet, but that's just because it hasn't grown up. You stay out of the other end where the saloons are, though, and there's nothing for you to bother that pretty head about."

"I certainly will avoid those areas, Sheriff. And thank you for not laughing at me."

"I never laugh at a lady, ma'am," Campbell said solemnly.

She smiled brightly at him and then set the half-full cup down on the desk and said, "Thank you for the coffee, too. I already feel better."

Campbell went with her to the door and let her out. He said, "I'd walk you back to the hotel, ma'am, but I got an important prisoner back there, and I can't leave right now."

"Oh, I'm sure I'll be all right."

"Tell you what. I'll stand here in the door and keep an eye on you until you get back inside. I can see all the way down the street to the hotel from here."

"Why, Sheriff," the woman's smile widened, "that's positively gallant of you!"

Campbell felt himself blushing. He kept his word and watched the young woman until she reached the door of the hotel. Then, as she opened it, she looked back and lifted a slender hand to wave at him. Campbell returned the wave with a sheepish grin and then closed and locked the door, glad he had been able to solve this little problem so easily.

He emptied the half-full cup of coffee the woman had left and rinsed the cup at the sink. Then he went back to his desk and his reading, finishing off his second cup of stomach-peeling coffee. It might be too strong for a lady, but it was exactly what was needed for a long watch.

He did not notice at first when the words in the dime novel started to get blurry. And by the time he slumped forward, his face against the rough wood of the desk, he was not aware of a thing.

Natalie ducked out of the hotel as soon as she saw the door of the sheriff's office close. Luckily, the clerk was still nowhere to be seen and would not be able to report her strange behavior.

Sticking to the shadows, she went toward the jail again. Disregarding Buck Campbell's advice, she hurried on past it and went down the street in the direction of the saloons. There were plenty of horses for the taking tied to the hitch rails in front of the drinking establishments. Careful not to be seen, Natalie untied one of them and led it up the street.

She tied the horse in front of the store next to the jail and then moved into the deeper darkness of the alley between the buildings. Then she waited. Standing beside the thick wooden wall, she shivered at the thought that her brother might be just on the other side of it.

She was sure that her plan would work. The spell of revelation she had cast in the hotel room had told her that her efforts this night would be successful. Flushed from the lovemaking, she knew that her powers had been at their height and that the message revealed to her had been true.

Drugging the sheriff had been simplicity itself. While he had not believed an intruder had tried to enter her room, he *had* believed that she was an overwrought, highly anxious woman—just as she had intended—and in his efforts to calm her down had been paying no attention at all when she dumped the minute amount of powder into his coffee cup. He would not taste or smell the potion, but it would do its work quickly.

And then soon, Sonora Pike—whom she knew and loved as Arthur Ingram—would be free, free to be reunited with the sister who had been searching for him for years. Waiting in the shadows, Natalie allowed herself to fantasize briefly about that reunion. Would he take her in his arms and hug her tightly as he had those many years ago? Natalie hoped so. She had been looking forward to this moment for so long.

When she judged that enough time had passed, she went to the door of the office and knocked again, calling out softly to the sheriff. There was no response. She wished that she could see into the room, but the shutters were closed over the inside of the windows. When she knocked harder and still got no answer, she knew that she would have to risk opening the door.

Lifting her skirt, she took the long, thin piece of metal that was strapped to her calf and began working on the lock. It did not take long for her to defeat it. Less than five minutes later, she swung the door open and stepped quickly into the office, shutting the door behind her.

Her eyes flicked around the room, taking in the scene. All was quiet. The sheriff was slumped over his desk, motionless, his head resting near an open book. Next to his outstretched hand was the empty coffee cup.

A smile curved Natalie's lips. All had gone as planned.

She moved over beside the desk and bent closer to the sheriff, whose breath rasped in his throat. Natalie was glad she had not used too much of the powder. If the man had died, she would have been able to accept it as necessary to free her brother, but this way was better.

She scanned the top of the desk and did not see the sheriff's keys anywhere. They were probably in his pocket, she thought. She began searching his clothes, pushing him gently to one side so that she could reach into his pockets.

A moment later, she was rewarded. The full ring of keys was in the pocket of his pants. She pulled them out and went to the door leading into the cellblock.

There were at least a dozen keys on the ring. Natalie began trying them, and the third one opened the cellblock door. She went to the desk and picked up the lamp there. As she carried it into the cellblock, the glow reached into the cells and washed over the sleeping figure in the one on the right.

Natalie's breath caught in her throat. She stood there for a long moment looking at him, taking in the weather-beaten features, the coarse hair, the thick, powerful body.

He had changed some over the years, but she would have known him anywhere. He was sleeping restlessly, shifting around on the narrow bunk and occasionally muttering under his breath. Natalie had heard all of the horrible stories about him, and if they were true, then he would have plenty of things in his past to give him nightmares.

With a slight shake of her head, she put those thoughts away. The stories about Sonora Pike were lies. He might be an outlaw, but he was no monster. Not her brother Arthur, who had loved her and taught her so much.

"Arthur," she said softly. Pike twisted his head, but he did not open his eyes. She called his name again.

Pike came up off the bunk, his eyes snapping open, his muscles tensing for trouble. He exclaimed, "What—who—" When his gaze fell on Natalie, he stared in surprise and consternation. He took a deep breath. "What the hell do you want, lady?" he asked. "Where's the sheriff?"

He did not remember her. Even though Natalie had been expecting that, the knowledge was painful. But it had been a long time, and she was no longer the child she had been when he saw her last.

"The sheriff won't bother us, Arthur," she said.

Pike took an involuntary step backward, frowning fiercely at her. "Who told you that name?" he demanded angrily.

"I know you don't remember me, Arthur." She began trying the keys from the ring in the lock on the cell door. This time it took six tries before she found the right one. As the lock clicked and she swung the door open, she went on, "I'm your sister."

Pike's frown deepened as he cast his mind back over the years. Dumbfounded, he finally whispered, "Natalie?"

There were tears in her eyes as she nodded and rushed forward, throwing herself into his arms. Pike embraced her awkwardly. She knew he had to be in a state of shock, being reunited with the sister he had left behind on the family farm after all these years. She buried her face against his broad chest, content to be with him again.

Pike lifted a hand and stroked her hair. Then abruptly he lifted his head. "The sheriff?" he asked.

"He's sleeping," Natalie told him. "He won't bother us."

Pike released her and hurried to the door of the cell-block, peering out at the office as if he had to make sure for himself that Buck Campbell was no threat. Seeing the sheriff slumped over the desk, he grinned broadly.

"Good job, sis," he said. "You took care of him, all right."

With Natalie following closely behind him, he went to the desk and studied Campbell closely. He reached down, slipped the sheriff's pistol out of its holster, and cocked it. With the muzzle pointing at Campbell's head, he shook the sheriff by the shoulder. Campbell swayed back and forth limply and showed no signs of waking up.

"Damn good job. Don't know how you managed it, but I'm glad you did. How the hell'd you find me, anyway?"

Natalie started to answer, to tell him about her years of searching, but he waved off her words.

"Don't really matter," he said. "The important thing is that you're here and that you got me out of that lockup."

"I had to get you free, Arthur," she told him sincerely. "I couldn't stand the thought of you in some cage."

"You and me both, sis." He reached out and took her arm, pulled her close to him. His rough fingers stroked her cheek. "I always knew you'd grow up to be a beauty, and you sure as hell have. Thanks for showing up when you did, Natalie."

"Oh, Arthur . . . ." It was just as she had dreamed. Her brother loved her and was glad to see her.

He shook his head. "Forget that Arthur business. I'm Sonora Pike now, Natalie. Always will be." His grin was savage. "It's a name people are afraid of, and that's the way I want it."

"All right." She nodded. If that was what he wanted, it was fine with her. "What are you going to do now, Sonora?"

"Get the hell out of here. What else? Wish there was time to take care of that damn bounty hunter who brought me in, but there ain't."

"There's a horse for you tied in front of the store next door. I hope it's a good one. I stole it from the hitch rail at one of the saloons."

Pike grinned broadly at her. "My little sis has turned into a hoss thief, eh? Reckon it must run in the family." He laughed and turned back toward the sheriff, and the expression on his face became ugly. "This hick lawman actually thought he could keep me in his jail. I'll teach him to lock up Sonora Pike."

There was a knife in a sheath on Campbell's left hip. In a flash of movement, Pike jerked the blade out, lifted it, and then plunged it down into Buck Campbell's back. The

knife thudded home, and even in his drugged state, the
sheriff let out a groan of pain as Pike twisted the blade.
Blood spread rapidly around the wound, soaking his shirt.

Natalie's eyes widened in shock at her brother's unex-
pected brutality, but she did not make a sound. Pike was
still grinning as he straightened up and said, "There. Now
he won't be raisin' any posse and comin' after me."

The statement was logical enough, but Natalie had seen
Pike's eyes as he stabbed the sheriff, and she knew the
real reason he had done it. He had done it for the sheer
thrill of killing a helpless man.

"Got to say good-bye, Natalie," Pike told her, pulling
her into his arms again. "Wish we had time for a better
reunion, but I got to be ridin'."

"I . . . I understand. Good-bye . . . Sonora. Good luck."

He cupped her chin, and his lips came down on hers in
a hard, urgent kiss. "Maybe we'll run into each other
again sometime. Hope so."

"So do I."

Then he was gone, hurrying to the door and glancing
out to check the street before running to the horse she
had waiting for him. Natalie went to the door and watched
him vault into the saddle. With a wave to her, he dug in
his heels and galloped away down the street, vanishing
within seconds in the shadows.

There was a sharp feeling of loss inside Natalie. She
knew that he was right about the need to get out of
Bonanza City, but it was still hard to say good-bye to him
so soon after finding him again.

She glanced over her shoulder at the sheriff's body and
swallowed the lump in her throat. She had not intended
for him to die, but there was nothing she could do about
it. Pike had been justified in his actions, she told herself
sternly.

Now she also had to get away from here. As far as she
knew, no one had seen her around the jail tonight. There
would be nothing to tie her to Pike's escape and the
sheriff's death. She closed the office door behind her and
locked it from the outside. Then she headed back toward
the hotel. As she passed a dark alley, she threw the ring of

keys far down into it as hard as she could. That would
certainly delay any discovery of what had happened tonight.

When she reached the hotel, she peered through the
lobby window before entering. The clerk was back behind
the desk. Natalie frowned at the sight of him. She had
been counting on getting back to her room without being
seen. Perhaps there was another entrance in the rear of
the hotel. She cursed her carelessness in not checking on
that before she put her plan into motion.

Luck—or rather the dark spirit that she worshiped, she
decided—was with her. There was a rear staircase on the
outside of the building that led up to an unlocked door.
Natalie found her room with no trouble. As she slipped
inside, she saw that the candles at the five points of the
pentagram had burned down and gone out, but there was
enough moonlight in the room for her to see Kendrick
sleeping in the bed. He was snoring, deeply asleep, just as
he had been when she left.

Natalie went to the window, letting the silver wash of
the moonlight play over her body as she began stripping
off her clothes. Her mind was working feverishly, and she
knew that many hours would pass before she would relax
enough to sleep this night, if at all. Her job was not yet
done, even though she had freed her brother from his
captivity.

Sonora Pike wanted revenge on the bounty hunter, the
man called Rory Darson. He would have that revenge . . .
through her. And her own lust for vengeance would be
satisfied at the same time.

As she took off her dress, her fingers encountered something sticky on the fabric. Holding the garment in the
moonlight so that she could see, she rubbed her fingertips
over the small dark stain.

Blood.

Natalie smiled. It had to be the sheriff's blood. It had
been on Pike's hand when he hugged her, and he had
passed the stain on to her. It was still wet, sticky on her
fingertips.

She lifted her hand and wiped the blood on her neck,

smearing it down onto the swell of her breasts. A shiver
ran through her.

She had passed an important milestone this night. Despite her intentions, she had been the indirect cause of a
man's death . . . and it was not so bad after all. In fact, as
she rubbed her bloody fingertips against her hard nipples,
a throb of exhilaration ran through her. Her brother had
known all along, had understood the thrill of taking a
human life.

And now so did she.

Chapter Six

It was almost ten o'clock when Hannah Campbell stepped out onto the porch of her family's house. She was tired but wide awake, not ready to go to bed.

A day like this would make anyone weary, she thought. First there had been the last leg of the trip on the stagecoach and then the meal tonight topped off by the brawl between Rory Darson and Vern Simmons. She had helped Vern wash the blood off his face and sent him home. Then she had pitched in to help the other girls clean up after supper. By now she should have joined her sisters in collapsing after the evening's work.

But Hannah's mind would not let her relax. She kept remembering the way Rory's fists had pounded unmercifully into Vern, and the way Vern had provoked that beating. It could have been much worse, she knew. Rory probably could have killed Vern with his bare hands if he had wanted to.

He had stopped short of that. While Hannah was upset that the fight had started in the first place, she was grateful that Rory had regained control of himself in time.

She leaned on the railing of the porch and looked down the street toward the sheriff's office. Her father had left on his rounds quite a while earlier, and by now he had probably finished them and relieved Luke Warner at the jail. He had been upset by the evening's events, too, but after Rory and Vern had left, his only comment had been that Vern had been asking for trouble and had gotten it.

He might not like Rory's profession, but he seemed to have nothing against the man himself.

Hannah wished she knew how she felt about Rory Darson. The tragedies he had experienced in his life were enough to make anyone hard and cold, but there seemed to be something else underneath his flinty exterior, something warm and human.

Emily had certainly liked him, and that was one point in his favor. It was hard to fool a child. An adult might be taken in by a charming smile and a glib tongue, but not a youngster. When Hannah had tucked Emily into bed earlier, the six-year-old had looked up at her and said, "Mr. Darson will come back to visit us, won't he, Hannah?"

Hannah had hesitated before answering honestly, "I don't know, sweetheart. If he stays in town for a while, I think he might."

Now, as she listened to the noises of the night and breathed in the cool air, she found herself hoping that he would come back to visit. She wanted to get to know him better.

For the time being, though, she decided that a walk might be what she needed to ease her mind. She would stroll down to the jail and say good night to her father. That way she could see if he needed anything else before she went to bed.

She was not afraid to be walking down the street at this hour of the night. There was an occasional rider, and she could hear music and laughter coming from the saloons, but she was not worried about anyone bothering her. Bonanza City had the makings of a good town, and she hoped that the family would stay here for a while. They were used to moving quite a bit, as a result of Buck Campbell's profession, but he had started talking about retirement, about settling down here.

When she reached the jail, she tried the door and found it locked. That was no surprise, considering that there was a dangerous criminal back in the cellblock. Hannah rapped on the thick panel and called softly, "It's just me, Pa."

She expected her father to open the little peephole and look through it, but it remained closed. There was no response from inside. Hannah frowned and knocked again. Still nothing. "Pa!" she called, louder and sharper.

Something was wrong. She felt her stomach tightening with fear as her instincts began to scream at her. Somehow, she knew, she had to get into that office.

There was a spare set of keys in her father's desk at home. She could get them quicker than she could get Vern or Luke Warner to open the door. There was certainly no way she could break it down. With a last nervous glance at the door, she turned and started back toward her house.

She was running before she was halfway there.

Moving as quietly as she could, so as not to wake up her sisters, Hannah went into the house and found the keys in the desk. There was a pistol in the drawer, too, and she lifted it out, the weight of it unfamiliar and uncomfortable. The cylinder was empty, but she knew there were cartridges in another drawer. Loading the gun took only a moment.

Then, with the keys in one hand and the Colt in the other, she went back to the jail.

She missed the lock on her first try with the key, her nerves betraying her, but when she finally got the key in place and twisted it, the door opened. Hannah stepped through, lifting the gun with both hands.

Her mouth opened and the barrel of the Colt sagged as she saw the motionless figure at the desk. She stood still for a long moment, stunned into immobility. Then a scream tore from her lips. "Pa!" she cried. The gun slipped from her fingers and thumped to the plank floor, luckily not discharging from the impact. Hannah rushed to her father's side, her eyes widening in horror at the sight of his bloody back with the knife buried in it.

She screamed again and again, and it seemed that her shrieks would never stop.

Rory had passed by the saloons without going in. For some reason, after what had happened at the Campbells', a night of drinking did not hold any appeal for him. As he stalked back to the boardinghouse, he thought bitterly that if it had not been for that fool deputy, he would still be back there, enjoying himself.

When he was back in his room, he spent some time cleaning his guns. They did not really need the attention, but it was something to do. He was too wide awake to sleep, especially this early.

His hands performed the task without much direction from his brain, leaving his thoughts free to wander. He remembered how Hannah had gone to Vern Simmons's aid, how the other members of the family had looked at him after the fight. He grinned. At least little Emily still liked him.

The hell with it, he decided. It had been a long time since he had worried about whether *anyone* liked him. There was no reason to start now.

The town seemed to be quieting down. There was less noise coming through the open window to his left. A slight breeze stirred Ma Donohue's lace curtains. Rory finished cleaning his Colt and was slipping it back into the well-oiled holster when a scream suddenly split the night.

He jerked up from his chair, instinctively pulling the revolver from the holster. The cries were coming from down the street somewhere, and there was something terribly familiar about the voice.

It was a woman's, and Rory suddenly realized that it belonged to Hannah.

With the Colt still in his big fist, he slapped the door of the room open and plunged out into the hall, taking the stairs three at a time going down. By the time he reached the street, several other people had appeared and were heading toward the jail, drawn by the screams.

His long legs got him there first. He stopped in the doorway, pistol up and ready, and saw Hannah standing next to the desk. Her father was slumped forward in his chair, his head resting on the desk, and even from where he was, Rory could see the bloodstain on Buck Campbell's back.

Two strides took Rory across the room. He did not know what had happened here, but he knew he had to get

Hannah away from the gruesome sight. Tucking the Colt behind his belt, he reached out and put his hands on her shoulders, turning her and pulling her away from the desk.

He put his arms around her, and after a moment she buried her face against his chest as sobs began to shake her body. Rory grimaced, unsure what to do, and began patting her lightly on the back. After a moment, he reached down with his long arm and put his fingers against Campbell's neck, checking for a pulse.

It was small and indistinct, but it was there.

The sheriff was still alive. Rory looked up and saw the shocked faces of several townspeople as they crowded into the doorway. "Somebody go get the doctor!" Rory snapped. "Move!"

A couple of the men disappeared, and Rory could hear their running footsteps on the boardwalk. As he held Hannah, the meaning of his words seemed to soak into her mind, and she lifted her head sharply to look at him. "My father . . . ?" she whispered, the words catching in her throat.

"He's still alive," Rory assured her. "The doc'll be here in a minute."

With a strong arm around her shoulders, he led her over to a chair against the wall and sat her down. As he straightened, he slipped his gun out. "You stay right here," he warned her.

Hannah caught at his arm. "What is it?"

Rory gave a shake of his head and pulled away, turning toward the cellblock. The door was open. He covered it with the pistol as he approached and peered into the cells. What he had feared was true.

Sonora Pike was gone.

Pike had done this. Rory was sure of that. He did not know how the outlaw had managed it, but he was responsible for Buck Campbell's hideous wound. As Rory glanced at the sheriff's body, a bright flame of rage began to burn deep inside him. After a life of crime, this was one more black mark against Pike.

And it would be the last, Rory Darson vowed.

But there would be time to catch up to Pike later. Right now, the important thing was saving Buck Campbell's life.

Rory glanced at the bystanders again and said, "One of you go find Vern Simmons. He's got to know about this."

"I'll go," a man volunteered. "Vern's been wantin' to be sheriff for a long time. Reckon he may get what he wants now."

Rory glanced at Hannah and then glared at the man. The man must have realized how callous his comment might have sounded to the wounded man's daughter, because he gulped nervously and hurried away. It was obvious by looking at Rory that the big bounty hunter was not anybody you wanted angry at you, especially not now.

The doctor came bustling in a moment later, wearing coat and pants over a nightshirt. He took in the situation in a glance and then bent over Buck Campbell's still form. To Rory, he said, "You know anything about knife wounds?"

"A little."

"Then you know that blade's got to come out of there. But when it does, the bleeding's going to get worse. You up to helping me here, son?"

Rory looked at Hannah, sitting in the chair, stunned into silence, and then nodded to the doctor.

Rory moved over beside the man, and they went to work. Carefully, the doctor removed the knife from Campbell's back and then rapidly cut the shirt away around the wound, which had started oozing blood.

"He's lost a lot of blood already," the doctor grunted. He took a dressing from his bag and handed it to Rory. "Put some pressure on the wound."

Rory did as he was instructed. When the bleeding had slowed, the doctor examined the injury and then swabbed alcohol on it.

"Can't tell what that blade hit when it went in," he said bleakly. "Might've punctured a lung."

Hannah's voice, close beside Rory, asked, "He's going to be all right, isn't he?"

Rory turned to her. He had not noticed her getting up from the chair. Although her face was pale, she had stopped crying and regained her composure. Rory met her solemn gaze and said, "Your pa's a mighty tough man. Reckon he'll pull through if anyone can."

"Not if we stand around gabbing about it," the doctor snapped.

"What can I do to help?" Hannah asked.

Her strength and bravery were impressive, Rory thought as she pitched right in, following the doctor's orders. Most women would have been completely shattered by such a horrible experience.

A few minutes later, while the three of them were still working desperately over Buck Campbell, Vern Simmons appeared in the door, his face bruised and haggard. There was a gun in his hand, and as he stopped, he lifted the weapon and pointed it at Rory. His thumb drew the hammer back. "Hold it, bounty hunter!" he barked.

Rory glanced up at him and frowned. "What the hell's the matter with you, boy? Put that gun down."

"No, sir," Vern said resolutely. "Somebody told me that Campbell had been hurt and that you were in here. I want to know what you did to him, Darson."

Hannah stared at the young deputy in disbelief. Finally, she said, "My God, Vern, Rory didn't do this! He came to help me when I found my father and screamed."

Without looking up from his work, the doctor added, "You're a medical man, are you, Vern?"

Vern frowned. "What? You know better than that, Doc."

"Then get your carcass out of here," the doctor snapped.

Slowly, Vern uncocked the pistol and put it back in its holster. He began tentatively, "I just thought—"

"No, you didn't," Rory cut in. "And you didn't notice that your prisoner is gone."

"Pike?" Vern hurried past them to the cellblock, staring through the door into the empty cubicles. "He's escaped!"

Rory grimaced and said, "If you want to do something to help, Deputy, you could round up a posse to go after Pike. Chances are, he's the one who did this to the sheriff."

Vern's face darkened with belligerence again. "Listen, Darson, who the hell are you to be giving me orders? I'm the acting sheriff in this town."

"Appointed yourself mighty quick, didn't you?" Rory's

sarcasm was not lost on Vern, he saw. The atmosphere in the room was tense, edgy. He wanted to smash his fist into Vern's face a few more times.

The doctor turned away from the desk and began to rummage in his bag. As he did so, he said, "I don't care what you do, Vern, as long as you get out of here. I don't need you standing around and blustering."

Vern looked for a moment as if he were going to make some reply, but then he shut his mouth and shook his head. He started for the door, but a quiet word from Rory stopped him when he reached it.

"Deputy," Rory said, "the next time you point a gun at me, you'd damn well better use it."

Vern gritted his teeth and put his hand back on his gun, but then he sighed and went on out of the jail.

"Did you have to do that?" Hannah asked when Vern was gone.

"What?"

"Make him back down."

"Just telling him the facts," Rory said.

The night was long, and none of them slept. By the time the sun was rising over the Sangre de Cristos to the east, Buck Campbell was bedded down in the doctor's spare bedroom, his condition serious but stable. He had not regained consciousness since the attack.

In the parlor outside the bedroom, three bone-tired people looked at each other, and the doctor said gently, "I think he'll make it, Hannah. There's no guarantees, but he's strong, and there didn't appear to be too much major damage."

"Thanks, Doc." Hannah looked as if she were about to drop.

Rory put his hand on her arm. "You'd best go get some sleep," he told her, and the doctor agreed.

"I . . . I have to take care of the girls," Hannah protested.

"I sent word to Mrs. Ballinger," the doctor said. "She said she'd look after them." To Rory, he added, "She lives next to the Campbells. Fine woman."

"I'm sure she is." Rory suddenly tightened his grip on Hannah's arm as she swayed slightly, drained and exhausted. "Come on, Hannah. No arguments."

She smiled tiredly. "All right. No arguments."

Hannah leaned on him as they left the doctor's house and started down the street. As worn out as he was, Rory knew it had to be worse on her. It was her father who had nearly been killed, who might die yet from his injuries. He was just glad he had been around to help.

It was amazing how quickly things could change, he reflected. Twenty-four hours earlier, he had not even known this young woman, and now some bonds had formed between them that might never be broken.

Three of the townspeople stopped them as they walked to ask how the sheriff was doing. Rory handled their questions, and as he did so, it became clear to him just how highly these settlers valued their sheriff. Buck Campbell was a well-liked man. That was only what he deserved, Rory thought.

When they reached the Campbell house, Rory saw that several women were standing on the porch. As he and Hannah climbed the steps, they gathered around to express their worry and sympathy. "Don't you worry about a thing, Hannah," a stoutly built young woman with blond braids said. "You've got plenty of friends here in Bonanza City. We'll take care of everything."

"Thanks, Ellen," Hannah replied, exchanging a brief hug with the woman. She turned to Rory and said, "Mr. Darson, this is Ellen Harwood. She owns one of the cafés here in town."

Rory nodded. "Pleased to meet you, ma'am. Reckon you could talk Hannah here into getting some rest?"

Ellen smiled at him. "I think I can, Mr. Darson."

"And if she can't, I'll see to it," a tall woman with a stern face said as she emerged from the house. "Your sisters are fine, Hannah," she went on. "They're worried about Campbell, of course, but I've convinced them to eat some breakfast. I want you to do the same, and then go to bed."

Hannah smiled. "All right, Mrs. Ballinger. I'm too tired

to argue with anyone." She turned back to Rory for a
moment. "You'll come by later, won't you?"

"Soon as I get a chance," he promised. Being on this
porch full of women was starting to make him nervous.
Despite the weariness he felt, the sense that he needed to
be doing something was nagging at him.

He nodded to Hannah and the other ladies and left the
porch, starting back down the street toward the boardinghouse. He planned to return there and pick up his hat and
holster, but he was unsure how to proceed after that.

On the way, Rory noticed that the door of the sheriff's
office was open. With a frown on his face, he swerved in
that direction and stepped up on the boardwalk on that
side of the street. He paused in the doorway, his eyes
narrowing coldly as he saw Vern Simmons sitting behind
the desk.

"You still here?" Rory asked.

Vern glanced up and returned Rory's glare. "Where did
you expect me to be?"

"Thought I told you to take a posse after Pike."

Vern laughed shortly. It was an ugly sound. "I don't
take orders from a damn bounty hunter," he snapped.
"Folks around here are peaceful. They're family men. I
can't ask them to go after a desperado like Sonora Pike and
maybe get themselves killed."

"What about you?" Rory demanded. "You're a lawman—
it's your job."

"You don't expect me to go after Pike by myself, do
you?"

Rory rubbed his jaw, seething inside. He knew damn
well that despite his bluster, Vern Simmons was too scared
even to try to track down Pike. Harshly, Rory said, "That's
what I intend to do."

As he turned toward the door, Vern hastily pushed his
chair back and hurried across the room. He reached out
and grabbed Rory's arm. "Wait a minute! Pike was in our
custody. You can't—"

Rory jerked his arm free and faced Vern with a deceptively calm expression on his face. "The hell I can't," he

said softly. "You won't bring him back, so that leaves it up to me."

Vern stared thoughtfully at him for a few seconds and then said, "I understand. Your reward money flew the coop last night. That's why you're going after Pike."

To his surprise, Rory realized abruptly that he had not even considered the effect Pike's escape would have on the bounty money due him. That was unusual for him, and another indication of the way his brief stay in Bonanza City had started to change him without his even knowing it.

"You believe what you want to, Simmons," he said slowly. As he stalked out the door, he threw over his shoulder, "I'll be back with Pike."

Bystanders got out of his way as he strode toward the boardinghouse. He supposed he looked pretty grim. He kept remembering the heartrending sound of Hannah's screams and the way Buck Campbell's body had looked. Despite the friction between Campbell and him, he had instinctively liked the burly sheriff. There was no way he could let Pike get away with what he had done. Rory had not been able to figure out how Pike had managed the escape, but that did not matter. What was important was getting on the trail before it got too cold.

When he reached the boardinghouse, he had to spend a few minutes filling in Ma Donohue on what had happened. She shook her head and clucked her tongue, saying, "Somebody should do something about that awful outlaw."

"I intend to, ma'am," Rory promised her.

It did not take him long to gather up his gear. He asked the widow to hold his room for him and then headed for the stable to pick up the horse that had originally been Pike's. He saddled up and headed down the street, intending to check the area around the jail for tracks. Rory knew that picking up the trail was not going to be easy, since there had already been enough traffic on the street this morning to wipe out most signs of Pike's flight.

As he reined up in front of the sheriff's office, he saw a lanky cowboy on the boardwalk arguing with Vern Simmons. "You got to find that horse, Deputy," the cowhand was saying. "If I go back to the ranch without him, the boss'll take it out of my hide."

"Look, Newt, I've got more to do than look for your nag every time it wanders off," Vern said self-importantly. "I'm the acting sheriff now, you know."

"Then why in hell don't you act like a sheriff, Vern?" the man demanded angrily.

Vern glared at him. "You'd better move along before I run you in for disturbing the peace, mister. Your horse just slipped loose from the hitch rail and found himself some grass somewhere. Why don't you just go look around for him?"

The cowboy shook his head disgustedly. "I tell you he was stole last night," he muttered. He spat in the street and then walked away shaking his head.

Rory had been paying close attention to the conversation. Ignoring Vern, he spurred his horse into motion and drew up alongside the upset puncher.

"I heard what you were telling the deputy back there, mister," he said. "Could I talk to you for a minute?"

The cowboy stopped and looked up at Rory with a suspicious frown. "You know somethin' about what happened to my hoss?"

"I might. You said somebody took him last night?"

Newt nodded. "I was down at the saloon cuttin' the dust, and when I come out, he was gone."

"You happen to know what time that was?"

The cowboy stuck his tongue in the corner of his mouth and thought. "Weren't real late," he finally decided. "Nine or ten o'clock maybe."

"Before the ruckus at the sheriff's office?"

"Just a minute or two before, now that I think about it."

Rory nodded. The theory that was growing in his mind had just about been confirmed. If he could get one more stroke of luck . . . "Is there anything unusual about that horse of yours, mister?" he asked.

"He ain't mine. Belongs to the spread I ride for. That's why I'm so worried about losin' him. He ain't worth much, but the foreman will still hold me responsible. But as far as anything unusual . . ."

Rory held in the impatience he felt.

The cowboy held up a finger. "You know, there is one thing. The shoe on his left back hoof is pretty near worn out. I been after 'em to replace it, but those yahoos I work with don't believe in fixin' nothin' till it's completely broke." He squinted and cocked his head. "You ain't said much, mister. You know who took my horse or not?"

"Reckon I might," Rory told him. "If I find him I'll let you know. Thanks, friend." Before the cowboy could say anything else, Rory kicked his horse into motion and started toward the edge of town.

There was no way of being sure that Pike had stolen the puncher's horse, but Rory thought it was a good possibility. Likewise, he could not know which direction Pike had gone, so all he could do was make his way around the edges of Bonanza City, looking for the distinctive tracks that a horse with a worn-out shoe would leave.

As he approached the Campbell house, he saw that the porch was empty now. All the women were probably inside. The door opened as he drew even with the house, though, and Hannah stepped out.

"Rory!" she called, coming quickly toward him.

She had used his first name, he thought, reining in. It sounded surprisingly good coming from her lips.

"I thought you were going to get some sleep," he told her.

"You were going to leave without telling me. You're going after Pike, aren't you?" Her tone was faintly accusing.

"Somebody's got to," he muttered, thinking about Vern Simmons's cowardice. Some people would consider it common sense, he realized. He said nothing about the exchange he had had with Vern in the sheriff's office.

"I started thinking about . . . what you might do, and I couldn't sleep." Hannah lifted a hand, as if she wanted to reach out and touch him, and then dropped it. "I won't try to talk you out of it. I just wanted to tell you to . . . be careful."

Her concern was obviously sincere, and Rory did not know quite what to say. After a moment, he told her, "I'll be careful. And I'll bring Pike back."

"If anyone can, I think it's you, Rory."

He nodded and then said, "Take care of your pa." Before she could say anything else, he spurred the horse into a gallop. He had some tracks to find—and besides, Hannah Campbell was getting just too distracting.

And having his mind on anything except recapturing Sonora Pike could get him killed.

From the window of her hotel room, Natalie Ingram watched as the tall bounty hunter rode out of town after talking to that little redheaded fool. Her fingers clamped down hard on the windowsill. She knew that Darson was going after her brother.

To her surprise, she had slept well. Kendrick had been gone when she had woken up this morning, but he had knocked on the door and entered not long afterward, bearing the news that he had picked up in the lobby downstairs. The notorious outlaw Sonora Pike had escaped from the jail during the night and while making his break had seriously wounded the sheriff with a knife.

"The sheriff's not dead?" Natalie had asked.

Kendrick had glanced at her sharply. "Not that I know of," he replied. "The word around town is that he's expected to live."

Natalie did not know how to react to that. The night before, she had accepted Campbell's death. In fact, the spilling of blood had seemed to intensify the power she had felt growing inside her. Now she was almost disappointed to hear that he was still alive.

Kendrick had asked her to come down to breakfast with him, but she had refused. "You go ahead," she had told him. "I'm just not hungry."

"You're sure?" His tone had been curt; he had seemed a little angry with her.

"I'm sure."

"You'd think you could have breakfast with your *cousin*."

Natalie had suppressed the irritation she had felt at his sarcastic words. "Please, Stefan, I just don't feel like eating now. I'd like to be alone for a while."

"Sure." He had gone out, but he had shut the door hard behind him.

He was so much like a petulant child sometimes. Natalie tolerated him because they had been together for quite a while, and he *had* been handy to have around from time to time. He planned their jobs and usually did so quite well. But soon the day would come when he would be dispensable. With the way her mystical powers were growing, soon she would not need anyone.

Now, as she watched Rory Darson leaving town, her anger at him grew until she knew she had to do something. She was wearing a silken robe, which she stripped off impatiently. Then, turning to the bureau, she opened the drawer and took out more candles and her chalk. Before going to bed the night before, she had rubbed the pentagram off the floor. It took only a moment to redraw it.

Even in the bright sunshine of morning, something about the ritual seemed to make the shadows in the room thicken. Natalie searched her mind for the proper words to chant, the spell that would call down doom and disaster on Rory Darson.

He would never recapture her brother. Never!

"What the hell is going on here?"

Natalie jerked to her feet as the harsh voice tore out behind her. She spun around and saw Kendrick standing in the doorway, a stormy frown on his narrow face. She had been so absorbed in her incantations that she had not heard him enter.

Fury gripped her as she blared at him, "How dare you! Never interrupt me during such a sacred moment! Never! Do you hear me?"

Kendrick grimaced and then snapped, "I hear you. I hear a lot of stupid mumbo-jumbo! I've warned you about this, Natalie. I've tolerated your superstitious nonsense."

"Nonsense? You fool! You don't understand—"

Kendrick took a long step across the room, and his hand lashed out, the palm cracking across Natalie's face and staggering her. "Shut up, you bitch! I won't have you talking to me that way!"

She stood stunned for a moment, holding her hand to the red mark on her cheek, and then launched herself at him, raking at his face with her long fingernails. Kendrick cursed and blocked her clawing hands away from him. Then he caught her with a backhanded blow that knocked her onto the bed.

His weight came down hard on top of her. "You slut!" he growled. "I'll teach you!"

She felt his arousal, intensified by the violence. Somewhere inside her, to her shame, she was feeling that same urgency. She tried to fight him off, but it was no use. Their coupling was almost as brutal as what had gone before.

She hated herself when the low, gasping moans of passion came unbidden from her throat.

When he was done with her, Kendrick picked up his hastily discarded clothes and began to dress. "In the future," he warned her, "you keep your mind on Winborn. We've still got a lot of work to do on him. I've got to go meet him and take that tour of his mine."

"Yes, Stefan," Natalie replied meekly.

He never noticed the hate in her eyes, the determination that things would be different someday . . . when all the secrets of the cosmos, of the dark netherworlds, would be hers to command.

Chapter Seven

Finding the tracks of the cowhand's stolen horse had turned out to be fairly easy for Rory Darson. After only ten minutes of searching, he had picked up the trail of a horse with a worn left-rear shoe. The trail led west, toward the rugged Cochetopa Hills, bypassing the other mining communities in the area.

Rory knew he was taking a gamble. There was no guarantee that Pike was the one who had stolen the horse. The thief could have been someone else, in which case Pike was probably getting farther away with every passing minute. But when he considered the timing of the theft, he sensed that he was on the right track—and anyway, he did not have anything better to go on.

As the day wore on and the terrain became rougher, Rory began to feel more at home. He thought wryly that Bonanza City had been making him soft, even though he had been there only a short while. Out here on the trail was where a man-hunter like him belonged. The life was hard and dangerous, but it was what he knew, and he had no doubt that he would track down Sonora Pike and apprehend him again. After all, he had done it before.

The only problem was, he kept thinking about Hannah Campbell and the way it had felt to sit down to supper with her and her family the night before. . . .

It had been a long time since he had slept, but Rory kept pushing on. He could not afford anything more than short breaks to rest the horse. Pike had a good lead, and the outlaw would probably be pushing his own mount to the limit.

That was going to backfire on Pike, Rory noted late that afternoon. He could tell from the tracks of the horse he was following that it was going lame. That bad shoe was to blame. If Pike had known about it, he never would have taken the horse, but Pike had been in a hurry, Rory figured, and had not paid close enough attention to what he was stealing. It was a lucky break, and Rory would take all of those he could get.

The ground was rocky, and it took all of the tracking skills Rory had developed over the years to stay on the trail. His shoulders ached with weariness, and he knew his horse was giving out. It would be easy to stop; he would have to anyway when night fell, and that was not far off. But he gave his head a shake. There was still light enough to read sign, so he pushed on, letting his anger at Pike fuel him.

He was riding up a long rise when he spotted movement ahead of him. The sun was just about down, which meant that the shadows were growing and a man's eyes could play tricks on him. But Rory had a clear view of a man on horseback topping the ridge ahead of him. He grinned. Pike was getting careless, letting himself be silhouetted against the sky that way.

Rory urged his horse into a faster pace. The going was too rough for a gallop, but Rory wanted to cut down the gap between him and Pike as much as possible. If he was going to catch up to the outlaw today, there was not much time left in which to do it.

He began to frown as he rode. That was not like Pike, letting himself be spotted on a ridge that way. Something was wrong.

Rory reached the top of the rise. On the other side, the hill sloped down to a tiny creek lined with cottonwoods. He saw Pike's horse disappearing into the trees, but the shadows were thick enough that he could not see Pike himself.

Suddenly his instincts screamed a warning, and Rory

left the saddle in a dive as a bullet whipped close by his head.

Pike had suckered him. He had known that someone was following him and had let himself be silhouetted against the sky just to draw the pursuer on. Then, as soon as he was out of sight over the ridge, he had dropped off his horse and hidden to wait in ambush for whoever was on his trail.

Those thoughts flashed through Rory's head in the split second before he landed heavily on the ground. As soon as he hit, he was rolling, not wanting to give Pike a good target. Another slug smacked into the dirt next to him, kicking dust into his eyes.

The ground fell out from under him. He dropped into a shallow gully—a stroke of pure luck, since he had not known it was there. But it gave him some cover and a few seconds of breathing space to blink the tears out of his eyes.

He slipped his Colt from its holster as he crouched there. Although there had not been time to think about it while it was happening, he had noted the direction the shots had been coming from. A quick glance over the top of the gully told him that Pike was probably forted up in a small stand of spruce about fifty yards away. Pretty long range for a handgun, but not impossible, Rory knew.

He kept his head up a little longer, trying to draw a shot, and sure enough a second later a rifle cracked. As Rory ducked, he felt the wind of the bullet. He had seen the muzzle flash in the trees and knew that his guess had been right.

He had Pike located now. All Rory had to do was disarm and capture the outlaw.

Rory grinned. That was going to be a pretty tall order, considering the circumstances.

The sun was gone, vanished behind the mountains to the west. Within ten or fifteen minutes, it would be dark. Then Pike would be able to slip down to the creek, find his horse, and take off again, and Rory would be unable to follow him.

Crouching low, Rory moved down the gully, a jagged scar down the side of the hill, cut there by millions of years of weather. As it became more shallow, he discarded his broad-brimmed hat, not wanting it to show above ground level. Part of the time he had to crawl on his belly, the sharp rocks on the bed of the gully gouging him.

There were a few more shots from Pike, none of them coming close. Rory wondered briefly where he had gotten the rifle. Buck Campbell's pistol had been missing, but no long guns were gone from the sheriff's office. Probably the rifle had been stored in a saddle boot on the horse Pike had stolen.

Rory was close to the creek now. He could hear the trickling of its narrow flow. A night breeze sprang up and soughed through the budding leaves of the cottonwoods. Somewhere nearby, a rock rolled.

Rory came up out of the gully in a rush, diving into the shadows beneath the trees. Orange flame blasted from a gun muzzle to his left, close, maybe twenty feet away. He snapped a shot in that direction and let himself fall as a return shot came. There was a rustle of brush, and Pike let out a harsh, involuntary curse. Rory heard hoofbeats and a splash. Pike was after the horse.

There was a two-foot bank at the edge of the stream. Rory came out of the trees and dropped off it, landing in the creek and holding his gun high to keep it dry. Just downstream, the horse came out of the woods, Pike right behind it grabbing at the reins. Rory tried to line up a shot, but the animal was in the way, between him and Pike. Pike latched onto the reins and jerked the horse's head around. Grabbing at the saddle horn with one hand, the outlaw found a stirrup and vaulted into the saddle. When Rory saw the barrel of Pike's rifle angling toward him, he squeezed the Colt's trigger, feeling it buck against his palm.

The bullet must have hit the barrel of Pike's rifle, because Rory heard the slug whine off into the gathering night. The outlaw cursed as the weapon flew from his hand. Rory could have fired again, but instead he closed the distance between them while Pike was groping for his stolen pistol.

Pike was not seated well in the saddle, and Rory took advantage of that by leaping up, the fingers of his free hand tangling in the outlaw's shirt. Pike fell from the horse, falling heavily into the creek, taking Rory with him. Rory slammed his left fist into Pike's face and then cracked the barrel of his Colt across the outlaw's wrist as he finally succeeded in pulling the pistol from behind his belt. Pike yelped in pain and dropped the gun. Rory hit him again, driving his face under the surface of the shallow stream. He put a knee in Pike's middle and held him there. Then he grabbed Pike's hair and yanked his head back up.

Rory jammed the muzzle of the Colt against Pike's jaw and drew back the hammer. Even over their splashing, Pike must have heard the gun being cocked, for suddenly he stiffened and was very still.

"Go ahead," Rory told him, his voice flat. "Keep fighting."

Pike was panting, his breath harsh in his throat. He said, "You . . . you got me . . . Darson. I won't give you no trouble."

Rory got his feet under him and stood up, keeping the gun against Pike's jaw. He took hold of the outlaw's shirt and hauled him up. "Come on," he ordered. "We've got to round up those horses."

He had been more than a little lucky again—Rory knew that. But a big part of luck was being prepared to take advantage of it. While the outlaw chased down both horses, Rory kept his gun trained on Pike, and then he retrieved Buck Campbell's pistol from the creek where Pike had dropped it. The rifle was useless, its action smashed by Rory's bullet. As he had speculated, it had been on the horse that Pike had stolen.

"You're not much of a horse thief, Pike," Rory said when they were both mounted up. "You should've taken a minute and checked the shoes on the one you grabbed."

Pike grimaced but said nothing.

Rory stopped by the gully long enough to pick up his hat, and then they started back toward Bonanza City. But after they had covered a couple of miles, he called a halt. The going was too rough to continue in the dark. "We'll wait out the night," Rory said. "Climb down off that horse. Slow."

When they were both dismounted and had removed the saddles from the horses, Rory tossed the handcuffs to Pike and had him attach himself to his saddle. Once that was done, Rory took his rope and cast a loop on the ground. Following orders, Pike stepped into it, and Rory was able to pull it tight around his ankles without getting too close. Pike sat down hard as Rory jerked the rope.

Some people might have said that he was being overly cautious, but Rory did not think so. Sonora Pike had proved how dangerous he was by getting out of that locked cell and stabbing Buck Campbell.

He left Pike's other hand free until they had had a cold supper; then he wound a loop of rope around the outlaw's wrist and trussed him to a tree. Between the rope and the handcuffs, Pike could barely move. That was the way Rory wanted it.

"The least you could do, now that you got me hogtied, is give me a cigarette, Darson," Pike said bitterly when Rory was done tying him.

"Reckon I can do that," Rory replied. He took out the makings and rolled smokes for both of them, putting one between Pike's lips once it was lit. Rory moved several feet away and sat down, putting his back against a tree trunk and relaxing as much as he would allow himself to. Deciding to indulge his curiosity, he asked, "How the hell did you manage to get out of that cell, anyway?"

Pike's grin was ugly as he shook his head. "I ain't tellin' you nothin', bounty hunter," he said while holding the cigarette between his teeth. "What difference does it make? I'll swing for killin' that fat sheriff, no matter what I say."

"You'll swing, all right," Rory agreed, "but not for killing Campbell. Leastways I hope not. He was still alive when I left Bonanza City."

Rory could not see Pike's face very well, but there was enough light from the moon and stars for him to recognize surprise on the desperado's features. After a moment, Pike muttered, "I figured I killed him for sure."

"You came damn close."

Rory crushed out the butt of his smoke. During the desperate fight with Pike, there had been no opportunity to think about what the outlaw had done. But now that things were quieter, Rory was remembering the blood-stains on Buck Campbell's shirt and the way Hannah had screamed. Dead or alive, that was what the reward posters on Sonora Pike said. Pike was damned lucky Rory did not just shoot him out of hand and claim the bounty on his corpse.

Rory sighed. He would take Pike back to Bonanza City alive . . . if he could.

Pike did not cause any trouble during the night other than his constant complaining. By morning, Rory was tired of it, so after they had eaten their sparse breakfast, he moved behind Pike and suddenly stuffed a bandanna in his mouth, tying the gag in place with a piece of cord. Pike thrashed around and glared murderously, since there was nothing else he could do.

When his prisoner had calmed down, Rory unfastened the handcuff on Pike's wrist and put the saddle on the stolen horse. Then he loosened the rope on Pike's other hand and stepped back, quickly drawing the Colt and leveling it at Pike. "Untie your legs," he ordered. "Then get up on that horse."

Pike did as he was told, and then Rory had him put his wrist back in the cuffs, fastening them securely to the saddle again. The outlaw could not go anywhere now without taking the horse with him. Rory climbed into his own saddle and holstered his gun, certain that he could get it out quickly if he needed it.

They headed east, Rory riding about ten feet behind Pike. They made better time than Rory had the day before, when he had been forced to go slower to read sign. Even so, the trip took the biggest part of the day, and it was late afternoon when they rode out of the foothills and onto the main street of Bonanza City.

One of the townspeople on the boardwalk spotted them coming, and Rory heard the man shout, "It's Pike! The bounty hunter got Pike!" The townsman turned and ran down the street, spreading the news, and people began to emerge from the buildings, flocking into the street to witness the return of the man who had nearly murdered their sheriff.

Rory glanced over at the gagged outlaw and saw the fury and rage on Sonora Pike's face. Given the chance, the outlaw would have probably killed everyone in Bonanza City right now, especially the ones who were cheering his recapture and laughing at the sight of him, cuffed, gagged, and helpless.

Several of the townspeople greeted Rory by name and congratulated him on bringing back Pike. One man reached up, slapped him on the back, and exclaimed, "Reckon you're a hero now, Mr. Darson!"

That made Rory uncomfortable, and so did the throng of people around their horses. He had gone after Pike primarily to satisfy his own anger, but he had also had an investment to protect. No one would give him bounty money for an outlaw who had turned around and escaped. He certainly had not risked his neck so the citizens of Bonanza City could stage a little impromptu celebration like this.

As he and Pike approached the jail, the door into the sheriff's office opened, and Vern Simmons stepped out, apparently to learn the cause of the commotion. Close behind him was Hannah Campbell. As Rory looked over the heads of the crowd, his eyes met hers, and a broad smile broke out on her face.

Somehow, he thought, that helped make all the trouble worth it.

Hannah pushed past Vern and hurried into the street, coming up to Rory's horse as he reined in. She said something, but Rory could not hear her over the clamor of the townspeople. He swung down off the horse, and as he

did the press of the crowd forced Hannah forward so that
their faces were only inches apart. Rory asked, "What did
you say?"

"I knew you'd come back," Hannah replied. "I just
knew it."

Vern Simmons elbowed his way up to them. His face
still showed the bruises that Rory had given him two
nights earlier, and the glare he sent toward the bounty
hunter made it clear that he had not forgotten. Rory
nodded to him, reached up, and hauled Pike down from
the saddle. "Here he is, Deputy," Rory said.

"I'm the acting sheriff, and don't you forget it, Darson,"
Vern snapped. He took hold of Pike's arm. "I'll get this
man locked up."

Several of the bystanders volunteered to help, and Pike
was marched into the jail. Vern, as he left, threw one
more resentful glance back at Rory.

"Seems that Deputy Simmons likes me even less now,"
Rory commented. "Reckon he was hoping I might not
come back."

"Don't say that," Hannah requested. "Vern just doesn't
understand a lot of things."

Rory understood one thing for sure. He was glad to be
back in Bonanza City, regardless of what he had felt while
he was on Pike's trail. The sight of Hannah had made up
his mind for him.

The crowd around them had thinned out some, now
that Sonora Pike was back behind bars. Hannah put her
hand on Rory's arm and said, "Come along with me to the
doctor's. Pa wants to see you."

"He's awake?" Rory was glad to hear the news.

"Some of the time. Doc has been giving him something
for the pain, so he's sort of groggy. But he asked me to
bring you over there when you got back."

Rory turned toward the doctor's house, and Hannah fell
in beside him. "Does the doc think your pa's going to be
all right?" he asked.

"It looks as if he will. He's going to need lots of rest and
time to recover, but he should be fine."

That was a relief to Rory. Buck Campbell was a good man, much too good to be done in by a skunk like Sonora Pike.

Hannah went on, "Did . . . did you have a lot of trouble with Pike?"

"Enough," Rory said. "I caught up to him just before dark last night. He put up a fight. I reckon I was lucky in a lot of ways. I'd still be on his trail if he hadn't stolen a horse with a worn shoe. It went lame yesterday afternoon, slowed him down enough for me to catch up. I'd best take that horse over to the livery after I've talked to your pa. The cowboy Pike stole it from will want it back."

Doctor Madison was standing on the porch of his house as Rory and Hannah walked up. He nodded to the bounty hunter and said, "I gather from the uproar earlier that you caught Sonora Pike again."

"I brought him back," Rory confirmed.

"Alive or dead?"

Rory grinned. "Alive. It was a sore temptation to do it the other way, though."

"I'm not surprised, considering all the man has done. Well, come on in. Buck will want to know all about it."

Buck Campbell was lying on his left side when the three of them entered the doctor's spare bedroom. His eyes were closed, but he opened them immediately as their footsteps sounded on the floor. He seemed to focus first on Hannah, and then he switched his gaze over to Rory. "You get him?" he croaked.

"I got him," Rory said. He took off his hat, tossing it onto a dresser. "Pike's back in jail, where he belongs."

"Got to keep him there this time. . . ." Campbell's voice trailed off. He seemed to be having trouble staying awake. Rory guessed that was from whatever the doctor was giving him for pain.

"I don't reckon he'll bust out again," Rory said.

Hannah knelt beside the bed. "How are you feeling, Pa?" she asked in a soft voice.

" 'M fine," Campbell slurred. "Thanks . . . Darson. Hannah told me . . . you helped save my life."

"Doc here did most of it," Rory told him. He hooked a chair with his foot and drew it over beside the bed. Glancing at Madison, he asked, "Is it all right for Buck to talk for a couple more minutes, Doc?"

Madison frowned and then said, "I suppose a few minutes wouldn't tire him too much. But keep it short, Mr. Darson."

Rory nodded in agreement. There were some things that had been bothering him, and Buck Campbell might be able to shed some light on them.

"Do you remember anything about Pike's escape, Sheriff?" he asked.

Campbell's forehead creased in concentration, and Hannah glanced up dubiously at Rory. She probably thought he should wait until later with his questions, Rory knew, but he wanted to find out how Pike had gotten out of the jail. The outlaw was sure to try something again.

"It's all kind of . . . fuzzy," Campbell said after a moment of thought. "Can't quite remember. I think I was reading and having a cup of coffee. . . ."

That much was true. Rory recalled the dime novel and the empty coffee cup on the sheriff's desk. He said, "What about Pike? Was he in his cell?"

"Yeah. I checked on him . . . when I sent Luke home."

"Did anybody else come to the jail that night?" Rory had been toying with the idea that Pike might have had help in his escape.

"Don't know . . . don't recollect anybody else being there. . . . It's all so jumbled up in my head." There was a fine sheen of sweat on Campbell's face as he tried to dredge the details of that night out of his memory.

The doctor leaned forward with a stern look on his face. "That's enough for now, Mr. Darson," he said in a tone that allowed for no argument.

Campbell went on as if he had not heard the doctor's words. "Pike must've got his cell door open somehow . . . hit me on the head from behind. . . . I never heard nothing. Next thing I know, I'm waking up here."

Rory nodded and stood up, snagging his hat from the

dresser. "That's fine, Sheriff," he said. "You just get some rest now."

"You . . . come back later," Campbell murmured. "Gotta talk to you. . . ." His eyes closed.

"Sure, Sheriff," Rory promised. "I'll come back."

As the doctor ushered Rory from the room, Hannah said, "I'll be right out. I want to sit with him for a minute."

When the door into the bedroom was closed, the doctor asked Rory, "Were all those questions necessary, Mr. Darson?"

"Pike got out of that jail some way," Rory replied. "I don't want him doing it again. If he's got an ace up his sleeve, we need to know about it."

"I expect that's Vern Simmons's worry, isn't it? He's the acting sheriff, after all."

Rory did not trust himself to respond to that right away, considering his opinion of Vern's abilities. After a moment, he said, "About that acting sheriff business, is that official?"

"Well, not really. The town council hasn't taken any action to appoint him to the post officially, and Buck hasn't said anything about it, of course. But someone must be responsible for law enforcement around here until Buck is on his feet again. Vern is the logical choice."

That might be, Rory thought, but logical did not always mean best. He kept that to himself, and a minute later the bedroom door opened again and Hannah came out. "He's asleep again," she said.

"Best thing for him right now," the doctor told them. "By tomorrow I should be able to decrease the painkilling medication. Then he'll be more alert and you can talk to him, Mr. Darson, as long as you don't wear him out."

"Thanks, Doc." Without really thinking about it, Rory took Hannah's arm, and they left the house. When they reached the street, he said, "I'll walk you home."

"Thank you," she replied quietly. "I'd like that."

They walked toward the Campbell house in silence. The crowd around the jail was gone now, but the sensation caused by Pike's return had not yet died away. Rory and Hannah passed several small clumps of townspeople who were discussing the outlaw's escape and recapture. Business in the saloons was booming, even though it was still daylight.

There was something natural about Hannah's arm being linked with his, Rory thought. He had always avoided romantic involvement because of the type of life he led. Saloon girls were always available to take care of his physical needs, and emotion had never played a part in that. But he had never met anyone quite like Hannah Campbell, either. Even though they had gotten off to a rocky start—because he was a bounty hunter—she seemed to be reconsidering her position, just as he was.

"I want to thank you, too," she suddenly said. "My pa was right. You did help save his life. And you brought Sonora Pike back."

"I wanted that bounty money," Rory replied with a grin. "I couldn't get it unless Pike was in jail."

"That wasn't the only reason." There was no doubt in Hannah's voice.

"No," Rory admitted. "I reckon it wasn't. But it was part of the reason."

"There's nothing wrong with a man wanting what's coming to him."

"Even a bounty hunter?" Rory's voice was harsher than he intended it to be. He felt the muscles of Hannah's arm stiffen and was suddenly afraid he had said too much.

Hannah hesitated and then said, "Anyone can misjudge a person. It's very easy to do."

"I suppose it is. I'm sorry—"

"Don't be. I'm very glad you came to Bonanza City, Mr. Darson."

He stopped and looked down at her. "You said you'd call me Rory."

Hannah smiled, and he knew the friction had been smoothed over again. "So I did . . . Rory."

As they walked on to her house, twilight was starting to settle in. They paused at the porch steps, and Hannah turned to him and asked, "You'll stay for supper, won't you?"

Rory grinned crookedly. "Your sisters didn't seem to be too happy with me the last time I left here, 'cept for little Emily."

"They know what you did for Pa. They'll all be glad to see you," she assured him. "Especially Emily."

"Well, in that case . . ."

Looking at her, at the way the breeze ruffled a loose strand of hair against the soft skin of her neck, Rory knew what he was about to do. He also knew that he probably should not do it, but there was nothing he could do to prevent it. He drew her into his arms and kissed her.

She responded coolly at first, as his lips came down on hers. It was bad policy, Rory realized, to kiss a gal right out in public. But as his arms tightened around her slender body, her mouth moved against his and then her hands suddenly clutched the back of his shirt. Hannah's eyes were closed as she pressed her body against his, eager and impassioned.

A hand clamped down hard on Rory's shoulder, jerking him back and spinning him around. Instinct took over at the first touch, and by the time Rory was facing Vern Simmons, his Colt was out and cocked and only inches away from the startled deputy's heart.

"Hold on!" Vern exclaimed nervously.

"Rory, don't!" Hannah said.

His face grim, Rory carefully let the gun's hammer down and then holstered it. "That was a damn-fool stunt, boy," he said coldly. "Coming up behind a man like that's a good way to get killed."

Now that the immediate threat was over, Vern's face took on its usual arrogance. "Just what the hell is going on here?" he said.

"Reckon that should be plain," Rory told him with barely controlled anger.

"I saw you going by the jail, and I wanted to talk to Hannah. Now I find you molesting her!"

"He was doing no such thing, Vern," Hannah protested. "He was just—"

"Just kissing you!" Vern snapped. "A damned bounty hunter." He ignored the warning looks he was getting from both of them and drew a deep breath. "All you've done since you got here is cause trouble, Darson. I want you out of my town!"

Rory saw Hannah's eyes flash with anger. "This isn't your town, Vern," she told him. "You're not the sheriff."

"I'm taking over as long as Buck can't do the job," he insisted.

"You say that like you intend for it to be permanent," Rory said slowly.

"We'll see about that."

Hannah said, "We certainly will."

"I don't want any trouble with you, Simmons," Rory said. "But I'm staying in Bonanza City, at least until my money gets here and Pike's on his way to Denver with some federal marshals. You got any objections, you'd better back 'em up with legal reasons. I'd like you to tell me just what laws I've broken."

Vern stared angrily at him. The determination was evident in Rory's voice. Finally the deputy said, "All right, but I'm putting you on notice, Darson. You'd best watch your step around here, or I will have you in jail."

He turned on his heel and stalked off, his neck stiff.

Rory and Hannah watched him go. "I'm sorry about Vern," she said. "He had some idea that he and I . . . that we . . ."

Rory shook his head. "No need to say anything else. Now, why don't we go see about that dinner you offered me?"

Like nearly everyone else in Bonanza City, Natalie Ingram's attention was drawn by the commotion when bounty hunter Rory Darson returned with Sonora Pike as his captive. Natalie was standing in front of the mirror in her room, wearing only a scanty black chemise, skillfully applying her makeup for the dinner date she had with Odell Winborn, when she heard the shouting from the street.

She went to the window and glanced out, unsure of what
was being said. She saw the two men riding into town—

And she froze in horror at the sight. There was her
brother, gagged and handcuffed, humiliated. Riding behind him was Rory Darson.

For a moment Natalie felt as though she had taken leave
of her senses. The room spun around her. It could not be!
She had called down curses on Rory Darson, cast spells
that should have ensured that he would fail in any effort to
recapture Pike. Yet here was the evidence before her own
eyes; she was the one who had failed.

She spun away from the window and went to the bed,
pulling one of her bags from beneath it. Forgotten was her
dinner engagement with Winborn. The scheme that she
and Kendrick had been working on for the last two days
was no longer important to her. She opened the bag and
took out a large, ornately bound book, handling it carefully, as if it were a loaded weapon.

In a sense it was, she thought. She had picked up the
mystical tome in a small, dingy bookshop back east. The
proprietor, a short, evil-looking man with a scraggly beard,
had leered at her and immediately tried to raise the price
when he saw how much she wanted it. Considering what
it was, she would have paid almost any amount of money
for it, and it had proven its worth time and again since
that day.

The spells in this book were powerful, so powerful that
she used them only when it was absolutely necessary, lest
the forces she was summoning up should turn on her. To
have her vengeance on Rory Darson, she would take that
risk.

She did not notice the time passing as she pored over
the arcane incantations in the ancient volume. Just thinking about some of the things she might be able to conjure
up made her soul shudder. But Rory Darson deserved the
worst she could do.

Finally, undecided as to what path to take for the moment, and weary from her studies, Natalie stood up and
went to the window again. As fate—or some other, darker

power—would have it, she saw Rory Darson and that Campbell girl walking together down the street. Natalie watched as they stopped and the bounty hunter took her in his arms and kissed her. Natalie seethed. He was so unconcerned, so preoccupied with himself and the red-head, void of any regret for what he had done to her brother.

Since Rory Darson was so fond of Hannah Campbell, that might be the way to strike back at him, Natalie mused. She wanted the bounty hunter to hurt, as she had hurt at the sight of her brother in a cage. She found herself thinking only of ways to have her revenge on him, rather than trying to figure out how to help Pike escape again. Her lust for vengeance had grown completely out of proportion, had become an obsession—and even if she had been aware of that fact, she would not have cared.

She turned back to the dresser where the magical book lay, just as the door opened and Stefan Kendrick stepped into the room. He took in her state of undress and the heavy volume spread open on the dresser, and his lean face turned a dull shade of red. "Dammit!" he exploded. "What the devil are you doing, Natalie?"

"You may not speak to me in that manner, Stefan," she said coldly. "You do not know what you are saying."

"The hell I don't. I know what I'm saying, and I know what I'm seeing. You're wasting time with that black-magic claptrap when you should be getting ready to seduce Winborn!" He took a quick step across the room and grabbed her upper arm, his fingers digging cruelly into her flesh. "Or have you forgotten why we're really here? There's a little matter of a gold mine!"

Natalie jerked away from him. "That mine is all you think about," she accused. "You don't care about me at all!"

"That's not true," Kendrick insisted, lowering his voice to a more reasonable level. "It's just that things are going so well with Winborn. Within a few days, he'll be ready to hire me as his new operations manager . . . if you keep him happy in the meantime. You know how much we can take from his business once I'm in a position of power."

"Yes," Natalie returned bitterly. "As long as I continue to play the whore for you and keep Winborn's mind off what is really happening."

A smug smile played over Kendrick's features. "Well, my dear, do you know a better role for which you're suited? You are a slut, you know."

"No!" Natalie's hand flashed up to slap him, but he moved too quickly for her. He caught her wrist, twisting it.

"Yes," he insisted, enjoying his domination of her. "A whore and a slut who has lain down for more men than you could ever possibly remember." He pulled her against him, keeping his hold on her arm and using his other hand to cup the firm, fleshy globe of one buttock under the black lace. His mouth came down hard on hers, and Natalie jerked her head to the side, not responding to his roughness this time as she usually did. "Remember? You told me all about it," he went on harshly. "You even told me about what your *brother* did to y—"

She did not let him finish. Her knee came up hard, smashing into his groin. He let out a gasp of pain and shoved her away from him. Natalie laughed as he doubled over.

Kendrick brought a fist up, driving it into her face and knocking her back against the dresser. Natalie cried out, as much from shock as from pain, and as he started coming toward her, murder in his eyes, her fingers fell on the small pair of scissors she used to trim her long nails. She jabbed them at his face as he lunged at her.

Kendrick jerked back, blood welling from the puncture in his cheek. The point of the scissors had narrowly missed his eye. He held his hand to the wound, and when it came away bloody, he said in a tone of disbelief, "You're insane, Natalie. You're really insane!"

"Get out of here!" she ordered. "We're through, you bastard! You'll pay for your brutality. I'll put a curse on your precious mine! Even if you get your filthy fingers on it, it will be worthless! *Worthless!*"

Her dark eyes were sparkling as she spat the words at him. Sparkling with a growing madness . . .

Kendrick kept backing away. Despite his pain, he laughed. "What are you going to do?" he asked. "You can't go to Winborn and tell him what we were planning, not without getting yourself in just as much trouble as me. You'd better just calm down, Natalie."

"Get out!"

Kendrick opened the door and ducked into the hall, shutting it behind him with a slam. Natalie waited a moment, drawing deep, ragged breaths, until she was sure he was not coming back.

Then she turned to the dresser and rested her hands on the open book there. She could feel its power coursing into her through her palms.

The dark gods could have her. She no longer cared about that. As long as she evened all the scores first.

Chapter Eight

The Campbell girls flocked around Rory when he and Hannah entered the house. Forgotten was the altercation he had had with Vern Simmons two nights before. Since he had helped save the life of their father and then had gone after Sonora Pike, their opinion of the bounty hunter had improved considerably.

Hannah was able to sit back and let Bess, Dinah, and Melanie do most of the work. Supper was already prepared, and it was no trouble to set an extra place for Rory. Emily made sure she occupied the chair next to him.

The older girls wanted to hear about how he had captured Sonora Pike, though Rory tried to pass it off as nothing special or even particularly dangerous. Hannah knew better. She had seen the bruises on Pike's face when he and Rory had ridden into town.

"I wish you'd have shot the no-good skunk," Emily said after Rory finished telling a highly sanitized version of the pursuit.

Rory grinned down at her. "Here now," he said. "What way is that for a little girl to talk?"

"Pike hurt my pa, didn't he?"

"He did at that," Rory allowed.

"And he is a no-good skunk, ain't he?"

" 'Isn't,' Emily, not 'ain't,' " Hannah corrected out of habit.

"I reckon that's true enough," Rory said. "He is a no-good skunk."

"So what's wrong with wishing you'd plugged him?"
Emily asked, her face a mixture of innocence and puzzle-
ment.

Hannah tried not to laugh at the expression on Rory's
face. He might be an old hand at dealing with dangerous
hardcases, but a curious, determined six-year-old girl was
another matter entirely.

She could see weariness gripping Rory as they ate. He
had been two nights with little, if any, sleep, and it had to
be catching up to him. He had kept going this long only
because he was used to a hard, rugged life, Hannah decided.

She wondered what he looked like when he was asleep.
Did those grim lines in his face smooth out? He was a
handsome man when he smiled, but that was seldom.

She thought about the kiss they had shared outside. She
had sensed that he was about to draw her into his arms,
but until the time came she had been unsure how she
would react. Now she wondered if she had been too
shameless to return his kiss so ardently.

Because she was the oldest, she had always had so many
responsibilities. Since the death of her mother the load
had been even heavier. Hannah was the closest thing to a
mother that little Emily knew.

Caring for others had become Hannah's main concern—
until Rory Darson had kissed her and awakened needs and
desires she had not known she possessed. Even now, as
she looked at him sitting at the table surrounded by happy,
redheaded females, she felt those desires in the pit of her
stomach. She was a brazen hussy, she thought.

And right at this moment, she did not care.

Thaddeus Montrose's General Mercantile usually stayed
open until ten o'clock, but old Thaddeus was thinking
about closing early this evening. It was nearly eight now,
and there had been only one customer in the last couple of
hours, a woman who had come in, looked around for a
while, and then left without Thaddeus noticing, obviously
not wanting to buy anything. He was the only one working

tonight. It would be nice, for a change, to eat his supper before the middle of the night.

He sighed. The life of a small businessman was a hard one. Should he stay until ten, knowing there would probably be no more customers, or leave and risk missing a big sale?

Thaddeus was leaning on the counter at the rear of the store, near the door to the back room, where all the mining supplies were kept. As he mused on the question, one of the floorboards suddenly creaked behind him.

He frowned and started to turn around. Could he have overlooked a customer?

Something hard slammed into the back of his head as he straightened. The stout old man gasped with pain and grabbed the counter to keep from falling. Again the assailant hit him, driving him to his knees. With a low moan, Thaddeus Montrose pitched forward on his face. The sawdust on the floor probably would have tickled his nose if he had not been out cold.

The merchant's attacker went to the door of the storage room, opened it, and slipped inside.

As much as Rory Darson enjoyed the meal at the Campbell household, by the time it was over the only thing on his mind was the bed in his room back at the boardinghouse. It seemed as though weeks had passed since he had had a good night's sleep.

He pushed back his chair and stood up, looking around the table at the Campbell girls. "That was surely a fine meal," he told them. "I appreciate it, Miss Dinah, Miss Melanie, Miss Bess." He nodded to each of them in turn and then reached down to ruffle Emily's hair. "You, too, little missy."

Looking up at him adoringly, Emily said, "I'm glad you came back to see us, Mr. Darson. Hannah said you would."

Rory glanced at Hannah. "Is that so?"

Blushing slightly, Hannah said, "I told her you might come to see us again if you stayed in town long enough. That was before . . . everything else happened."

"Well, I'm mighty sorry about what happened to Buck," Rory said solemnly, reaching for his hat. "But I'm right glad I was able to pay all of you a visit again." He settled the hat on his head and turned toward the door.

Hannah rose and hurried around the table to join him. He saw the glance she shot at her sisters as the girls tried without success to hold in their giggles. Rory did not know much about young girls, but he would have been willing to bet that Hannah would get some sisterly razzing about being sweet on him after he left.

And she was sweet on him. Rory knew that from the way she had responded when he kissed her—knew it from the way she looked at him now as they went to the door.

In a soft voice, she said, "You'd better get some rest tonight."

"Reckon we could all use some. I thought I'd go by the jail first, check on Pike."

"Do you think that's a good idea? I mean, Vern will probably be there."

Rory looked into her eyes and said slowly, "I'm sorry if it causes trouble, Hannah, but I'm not going to let that young pup run me off. I've got a stake in Pike staying in that cell this time."

"I know you do," Hannah admitted. "I just don't want anyone else getting hurt."

Rory put a big hand on her shoulder and squeezed lightly. Her flesh was warm and firm under her blouse, and he kept his hand there a little longer than was necessary for the reassuring gesture he intended it to be. "Don't worry," he told her. "Nobody's going to get hurt. I think that deputy understands me now."

Hannah glanced over her shoulder at the other occupants of the room. The girls were clearing the table and pretending not to pay any attention to Rory and their sister. Rory and Hannah both knew that in reality the girls were avid spectators. When Rory moved out onto the porch, Hannah went with him, shutting the door behind them.

She turned her face up to him, and he kissed her tenderly, lingeringly. In a whisper she asked, "How did this happen?"

Rory shook his head. "Damned if I know," he replied, equally softly. "I'm just glad it did."

He let his hand slide down her arm until it reached her fingers. Smiling into her eyes, he held her hand for a moment. Then he released her fingers and turned to the steps. With a final glance he started up the street toward Bonanza City's jail.

The town still seemed to be celebrating Pike's capture. Quite a few people were on the street, and most of them had a friendly greeting for him. He certainly seemed to have risen in the town's estimation since his arrival, at least in most quarters. Vern Simmons would still not have a good word for him, he was willing to bet.

The door to the sheriff's office was locked. Rory rapped hard on the wood, and a moment later he saw the peep-hole cover swing back. A voice he did not recognize called through the door, "Howdy, Mr. Darson. Hold on a minute, and I'll let you in."

When the door opened and Rory stepped into the office, he saw no sign of Vern Simmons. The man who shut and relocked the door was young, tall, and gangling. This had to be the part-time deputy Buck Campbell had mentioned.

"Reckon we ain't been introduced," the young man said, extending his hand. "I'm Luke Warner. 'Course, I knowed right away who you was."

"Hello, Luke," Rory said, shaking hands with him. "Deputy Simmons around?"

"He went out for some supper. Should be back before too much longer, though."

Rory nodded. "Had any trouble with Pike?"

"Not a lick," Warner answered. He put his hand on his gun butt, as if the very mention of Pike made him nervous.

Luke Warner might be a pleasant young man, but Rory was not sure that he was a good person to be guarding Pike by himself. After all, the outlaw had escaped when Buck Campbell was on duty, and Campbell was tougher and more experienced than Luke Warner.

Rory jerked his head toward the cellblock. "Mind if I have a look at him?"

"Sure thing, Mr. Darson. He ain't doin' nothin', just sittin' back there. Reckon he's pretty upset over bein' caught and brought back." Warner swallowed, his Adam's apple working in his thin neck. "I know I'd be upset if I was on my way to a hangin'."

Rory grinned. "You and me both, Luke."

Warner took a ring of keys from a drawer in the desk and unlocked the cellblock door. He opened it and stepped back to let Rory go through first.

Sonora Pike barely glanced up when Rory stepped in. He was sitting on his bunk, a cigarette dangling from his mouth. Tonelessly, he said, "Come to gloat, bounty hunter?"

"Nope, just making sure you haven't tried taking off again," Rory replied. He studied the cell door, paying particular attention to the area around the lock. This was the same cell that Pike had been in earlier, before his escape. Rory was not sure that was a good idea, putting him back in the same cell, but he was not surprised that Vern Simmons had not considered that.

Nevertheless, the barred door and the lock looked secure enough. He rested a hand on one of the bars and said, "Is there anything I can do for you, Pike?"

The outlaw squinted at him, puzzled. "You offering to do something for *me*, bounty man? What the hell are you up to?"

"Not a damn thing," Rory answered sincerely. "Just figured it wouldn't do any harm if you had something to help pass the time. I could have a bottle sent over from the saloon."

Pike ran his tongue over his cracked lips. "Yeah," he said slowly. "That'd be right nice."

"I'll see to it," Rory promised. He saw Luke Warner frowning and knew that the jailer had to be doubting the wisdom of giving liquor to a prisoner. Rory had not made the offer out of the goodness of his heart, however. Chances were that if Pike started drinking, he would not stop until he had finished off the bottle. A dead-drunk outlaw would be less dangerous than an angry, stone-cold sober one.

When they were back in the office with the cellblock

door closed and locked, Warner said dubiously, "I don't know if Vern will allow a prisoner to have any booze."

"Is there a law against it?"

"Well, not that I know of."

"If the deputy has any objections, you tell him to come see me, because I take it personal when I'm not allowed to keep my promises, even to polecats like Pike."

Luke bobbed his head. "Sure, Mr. Darson, whatever you say. Vern is the acting sheriff, though. He don't like it when people call him a deputy no more."

Rory grinned. He knew that as well as Luke.

He said good night to the jailer and then went across the street to one of the saloons. The bartender there was shocked to hear that Rory wanted him to send a bottle of his best whiskey over to the jail for the prisoner, but Rory insisted and rattled his final coin on the bar. Things had been so busy, he had never had a chance to see about getting some kind of advance on that reward money. Maybe it would not be too long now before the marshals arrived from the state capital, he thought as he headed for the boardinghouse.

But when the bounty money finally did come, he was going to have a hard decision to make. There would be nothing stopping him then from drifting on out of Bonanza City. Nothing except Hannah Campbell.

Earlier that evening, Stefan Kendrick had met Odell Winborn in the lobby of the hotel. Winborn stood up when he saw Kendrick coming down the stairs, a frown creasing his face as he noted that Kendrick was alone.

"Hello, Odell," Kendrick said heartily as he came up to the mineowner and shook his hand. "I hope you're well this evening."

"I'm fine, thank you," Winborn replied. He looked up at the stairs again, as if hoping to see Natalie there, and then returned his disappointed gaze to Kendrick. "I thought your lovely cousin was going to join us for dinner."

Kendrick grimaced. "She certainly intended to. In fact,

that was all she talked about all day. But poor Natalie is a bit, ah, indisposed this evening."

Winborn drew in his breath sharply in concern. "It's nothing serious, I hope?"

"Oh, no, just a touch of something in this mountain air, I expect. She'll be fine by tomorrow, no doubt. I hope you'll still do me the honor of dining with me."

Winborn waved a hand. "Of course, of course. Say, do you think Miss Natalie would be up to having a visitor? It might cheer her up."

"Ah, I don't think so," Kendrick said hastily. He lowered his voice. "You know how women are, old boy. They don't ever want a gentleman to see them except when they're at their best. Especially *certain* gentlemen."

Winborn flushed with pleasure at the implication that he was special to Natalie. "I understand," he said, matching Kendrick's man-of-the-world tone.

Kendrick sighed quietly with relief. Winborn had believed the story. More importantly, he had believed the flattery. Kendrick was confident that he could keep the mineowner on the string long enough to make Natalie come to her senses. The woman seemed to be losing her grip on reality, but she would calm down when she realized how much money was riding on this deal, he reasoned.

As the two men started into the hotel dining room, Winborn gestured at Kendrick's face. "What happened there? Looks almost as if somebody went after you with a knife."

Kendrick lightly touched the wound Natalie had given him. "It was my own foolish fault," he said lightly. "I was trimming my beard and accidentally stabbed myself." He laughed. "I suppose I'm lucky I didn't put my eye out!"

"Nasty things, scissors," Winborn agreed solemnly.

Kendrick did not mention the ache in his groin. Natalie's knee had done more painful damage than the scissors she had wielded.

As the two men sat down to dinner, Kendrick did not even think about Natalie's threat to call down curses and make Winborn's mine worthless. He had never believed in her occult nonsense, and he certainly did not put any

stock in her threats. There were too many things that
could go wrong for reasons other than witchcraft.

Ma Donohue was still up when Rory reached the
boardinghouse, as were several of the men who lived
there. All of them wanted a chance to congratulate him
and ask him about Pike's capture. Rory tried to be polite,
but exhaustion had too strong a grip on him. He bid them
good night and headed upstairs to his room and the bed
that was waiting there.

Hanging his hat on the back of a chair, he stripped off
the shell belt and holster and put them on the seat cush-
ion. Once his boots were off, he did not bother disrobing
any further, but blew out the lamp, sprawled on the bed,
and let his head sink into the pillow. Almost immediately,
he was asleep.

There was no way of knowing how much time had
passed after he had dozed off when a loud rumble suddenly shook Bonanza City. Rory came awake instantly, his
hand flashing to the chair beside the bed and snagging the
Colt from its holster. He rolled out of bed, his eyes
searching the shadowy room and finding no threat. Echoes
of the sound that had disturbed his slumber were still
rolling through the hills surrounding the town, fading
gradually like distant thunder.

Shouts came from the street, and Rory went to the
window and pushed the curtain back, peering out to see
people spilling from the doors of buildings all up and
down the street. Most of them were looking toward the
mountains, and one man who came out of a saloon threw
back his head and bawled out the most dreaded cry in any
mining community: *"Cave-in!"*

Rory stood at the window for a long moment, watching
the townspeople scurrying around like ants. Others took
up the cry started by the first man. Rory did not doubt
they were correct. These were mining people; they would
know the sound of a cave-in when they heard it.

But was it any of his business? True enough, his affairs
seemed to have become tied to those of the town, but that
was through no choice of his own. Still, if a mine shaft had

collapsed, men had more than likely been hurt—they might even be trapped right now. Had he been so hardened by his life that he did not care about that?

He pulled his boots on hurriedly. Standing around thinking was not going to do anybody any good.

When he reached the street, he glanced toward the jail, and the thought occurred to him that if Pike did have an accomplice in town, this might be a distraction to mask another escape attempt. Rory hurried toward the sheriff's office, his hand on his gun butt.

"Who is it?" Luke Warner yelled when he pounded on the door.

"It's Rory Darson, Luke. You all right in there?"

"Just fine, Mr. Darson. Say, what's going on out there?"

"People are saying that there was a cave-in up at the mines."

"That's what I thought it sounded like," Warner replied. "I'd like to be able to help."

"No, just stay put," Rory commanded sharply. "Keep an eye on Pike."

Luke called out that he understood, and Rory thought the young man sounded glad to have someone else making decisions and giving orders, even if that someone was not Bonanza City's acting sheriff. Rory wondered briefly where Vern Simmons was.

He heard his name called and looked into the street, where he saw people hurrying by on foot, on horseback, and in wagons and carriages. A buckboard was drawn up a few yards away, and Hannah was at the reins, holding in the team of nervous horses. Sitting beside her was the young blond woman Rory had met at the Campbell house the morning after the sheriff was wounded. He remembered that her name was Ellen . . . Ellen Harwood.

Hannah was wearing a thick robe with the hem of a nightgown showing beneath it, and her hair was loose and rather disarrayed. Rory thought he had never seen her looking more beautiful.

"Can you come help us, Rory?" Hannah asked as he hurried over to the wagon. "There's been a cave-in up at the Vista mine."

Rory glanced at the crowd. "Looks like the whole town's going up there already."

"Everyone pitches in when there's trouble at the mines, Mr. Darson," Ellen said.

Hannah Campbell's presence was enough to make up Rory's mind. He did not want Hannah and Ellen going off with that mob by themselves. Vaulting up into the bed of the buckboard, he said, "Let's go."

Hannah flicked the reins and got the team moving again. They fell in with the steady flow of people moving toward the mine. Sitting in the back of the buckboard, Rory took off his hat and rubbed a hand over his face. However long he had been asleep, it had not been long enough.

The road became rougher and steeper as it left the town behind. Hannah seemed to be having trouble controlling the horses. After a particularly violent lurch of the wagon that almost took it off the road, Rory said, "You'd best let me handle the reins."

"I think you're right," Hannah said, somewhat shakily.

Ellen stood up carefully and stepped into the back of the buckboard, leaving room on the seat for Hannah to move over. Rory sat down beside her and took the reins, hauling the nervous team back into line.

He started to ask where the mine was located and then realized he could follow the flood of people. He asked, "Is this Vista a big claim?"

"Not as big as some of the others around here," Hannah answered. "It's a steady producer, though. It's made Mr. Winborn a rich man."

Rory nodded. He had heard Odell Winborn's name around town and knew that the man was respected and well liked. That was probably why so many of the citizens were flocking to help.

A blaze was visible in the hills up ahead, and as they approached, Rory could see that it came from a multitude of torches, rather than one big fire. The light from the torches revealed a mine shaft cut into the side of a rocky hill. Just below the shaft opening was a cluster of buildings.

Rory halted the wagon next to several others on a level spot below the mine buildings. He hopped from the seat and then helped Hannah and Ellen down. The three of them joined the crowd around the building where the mine offices were located.

Vern Simmons was standing on the steps leading into the office, putting him a couple of feet above the crowd. He waved his arms in the air and shouted, trying to make himself heard over the din. Somewhere a woman was crying, loud, jagged sobs that cut through the noise of the mob.

"Everybody quiet down!" Vern yelled. "We've got to get organized here! There are men trapped in that mine!"

No one seemed to be paying attention to the deputy. Hannah clutched Rory's arm and pointed to a man at the bottom of the steps. "There's Mr. Winborn! Maybe he knows what happened."

"You stay here," Rory said, and then he began making his way through the crowd. He shouldered people aside, drawing a few angry looks. When he reached Winborn, his hand fell on the mineowner's shoulder, and he said, "Come on."

Pulling Winborn along with him, he started up the steps. Vern Simmons glanced down, his face hardening when he saw Rory. Before the deputy could say anything else, Rory's voice roared out, sweeping over the crowd.

"Hold it! All of you, shut up!"

Silence gradually fell over the group. They looked up at Rory and Winborn. Rory turned to the man and asked in a loud, clear voice, "What's the situation in the mine?"

Winborn was pale with strain. He said, "The roof of the shaft appears to have collapsed. We're not sure how far into the mine the cave-in goes."

"There's men inside?"

Winborn nodded, his eyes reflecting the agony he must have been feeling. "I don't know how many, maybe as many as a dozen or more. I just don't understand what happened. I just don't know . . ."

The mineowner was so shaken up that he was not going to be of much help, Rory realized. He turned to Vern. "I don't know a damn thing about mines," he said in a low voice. "Reckon we'd better get busy doing *something*, though."

Vern glared at him. "I'm in charge here, Darson, and don't you forget it."

"Then do something," Rory responded, his voice flat and cold.

"All right," the deputy said, raising his voice and turning to the crowd again. "We've got to dig those men out of there. There should be picks and shovels over there in the storehouse—" He glanced at Winborn, who nodded in confirmation. "So let's go get started!"

The crowd surged toward the storehouse, and Rory, Vern, and Winborn went with them. Rory tried to spot Hannah again, but he had lost track of her.

The door of the storehouse was locked, but Winborn produced a key and opened it. Rory stood in the doorway while Vern and the mineowner went into the building and began passing picks and shovels to him. Rory handed the tools on to the men waiting to begin the rescue effort.

There were not enough tools to go around, but that was all right. It looked as if a long night of hard work was in front of them, and the rescuers would need to alternate stints of digging in the shaft. When Vern handed him a shovel and said, "That's the last of them," Rory nodded and hung onto it for himself.

He looked at the men gathered around the storehouse and realized that none of them had gone into the shaft yet. Their faces were turned toward him in the torchlight. With a shock, Rory realized that they were looking to him for leadership. He was an outsider, a stranger to most of these people, but they were going to follow his lead—whether he wanted that or not.

"Well, come on," he said, pushing through the ring surrounding him and striding toward the mine shaft. "Let's go get those men out of there."

When Rory heard someone rush up next to him, he glanced over to see Vern Simmons carrying a pickax. The deputy's face was set in hard, angry lines. Clearly Vern minded Rory's taking over the position of leadership, but he had enough sense to realize that now was not the time to make an issue of it.

Rory wished he knew what had happened to Hannah.

There were plenty of women around; he was sure she would be all right. But it would have been nice to see her again before going into that dark hole.

Even though the cave-in had happened at least a half hour earlier, the dust inside the shaft was still thick and choking. It drifted slowly out of the opening. Rory told several of the men who did not have tools to take torches into the shaft.

The first group of rescuers moved into the mine, following the men with the torches. The light they provided seemed to be swallowed up for the most part by the dust, but there was enough illumination for Rory to see the wall of rock that closed off the shaft about twenty feet into the mountain. There was no need for talking. All of the men knew what had to be done. Rory leaned his shovel against his leg for a moment and tied his bandanna around his mouth and nose to protect him from some of the dust. The others followed suit.

Then, with Vern Simmons beside him still looking irritated, Rory lifted his shovel and drove it into the barrier of dirt, rocks, and rubble.

That was the beginning of a hellish night. The tunnel was only wide enough for four or five men to work at a time, but the others behind them had their hands full keeping the shaft clear of the debris thrown back by the diggers. Coughing and blinking back tears caused by the dust, Rory raised the shovel and then sent it biting into the wall again and again. Blisters rose, even though his hands were hardened by work.

Rory knew little about this sort of labor, but luckily most of the rescuers were miners themselves. As they made progress, some of the men braced up the cleared section so that it would not collapse further. But they could not afford to spend too much time on the bracing. All of them were taking a chance just by being there, Rory knew. Another, more extensive cave-in was all too possible.

Rory's arms felt like lead when a man appeared at his shoulder and reached out to take the shovel. "Go take a break, partner," the man told him, grinning. "Give the rest of us a chance to have some fun."

Rory grinned bleakly back at him and handed over the shovel. The other members of the first group of diggers were being relieved as well. He and the men with him walked slowly back to the mine entrance.

The night air was cool and clean and sweet as Rory tugged off the cloth covering his face. He filled his lungs with it, letting it clear away some of his weariness. Down the mountainside, he spotted a long table that someone had found and set up. The women of Bonanza City were gathered around it, putting out sandwiches and coffee.

"Smell that java!" one of the men exclaimed in a hoarse voice. "Outta the way, boys!"

Rory looked toward the table and saw torchlight shining on red hair. A grin creased his face as he started toward it. Hannah was there with Ellen Harwood and the other women, handing out food and pouring cups of coffee for the men. She was so busy that at first she did not look up when he stopped in front of her. Instead, she thrust a cup and a sandwich full of thick slices of beef at him.

"Thanks, ma'am," Rory said.

Hannah glanced up at him, her eyes suddenly bright, and she reached out to touch his arm. "Rory," she said softly. "Are you all right?"

He nodded. "Just a little tired, that's all. And I reckon this food will help that a lot."

Her fingers tightened on his arm. He could feel their warmth through his shirt. "Go sit down somewhere and eat," she told him. "I'll come sit with you as soon as I get a chance. But right now . . ." She gestured toward the table.

"I understand. You go ahead with what you're doing."

He found a good-sized boulder and sat down with his back against it, stretching his long legs in front of him. Sitting down felt about as good right now as anything he had ever done. He sipped the hot coffee and took a big bite of the sandwich. His hands were throbbing with pain, but he tried to force that out of his mind.

When he was finished with the food and coffee, he put his head back against the boulder and closed his eyes. It was amazing how much the hard rock felt like a soft pillow.

He was not sure if he dozed off or not, but suddenly he felt cool fingers stroking his forehead. He opened his eyes and saw Hannah kneeling beside him. A few minutes earlier, her hand had felt warm, but now its coolness was refreshing and relaxing.

She smiled and asked again, "Are you all right, Rory?"

He nodded. "I am now."

"How is it going inside?"

Rory grimaced. "It's a hell of a job. From the looks of it, a lot of the tunnel collapsed. I don't think we're going to find anybody alive in there."

"I'm so sorry," Hannah said, shaking her head. "Everybody who has been around mines very much knows there's always a chance something like this can happen, but somehow you never expect . . ."

"I know," Rory said as her voice trailed off.

They sat quietly for a few moments, Rory taking strength simply from her nearness. Gradually, he became aware of someone else watching him. He glanced around and saw Vern sitting a few yards away, resting his back against a rock in a similar position. The deputy's grimy face was set in a glare.

Vern was just going to have to get used to seeing him and Hannah together, Rory thought. If he did not, sooner or later there was going to be even more trouble.

Rory saw Ellen Harwood walk up to Vern and hand him a cup of fresh coffee. He spoke briefly to her and then switched his attention back to Rory and Hannah. Ellen stood beside him for a moment longer. Then she turned and walked away.

Rory had seen the expression on Ellen's face, even from where he was sitting. Vern Simmons was blind as well as belligerent, he thought. That young woman had strong feelings for him.

"Guess I'd better get back in there," he said, pushing himself to his feet and extending a hand to Hannah.

As he helped her up, she said, "I think you should rest some more."

Rory glanced up at the stars, trying to calculate the time. Even though it seemed that he had been inside the mine for hours, he could tell now that it was probably only one or two o'clock in the morning. "It'll be a long night yet," he said. "Everybody'll have to take several turns."

Hannah walked beside him to the tunnel, where the other members of the first group were trooping back into the shaft to reclaim their tools. Rory squeezed Hannah's shoulder and sent her back to the table with the other women. Before she went, she said in frustration, "I wish I could go in there with you and help!"

"You'll do more good out here," Rory told her. "Keep that coffee brewing."

Once back inside, he found that several more feet of the cave-in had been cleared away. He made his way to the head of the tunnel, claimed a pick from an exhausted worker, and then began breaking up the tightly packed debris.

Somehow, Vern Simmons ended up beside him again. From the way Vern glanced at him every so often and then seemed to work harder, Rory began to understand what was happening. *That damn fool is going at it like this is some sort of competition!* he thought. Vern was out to prove that he could dig faster and farther than Rory. Rory snorted in disgust and kept plugging away, not paying any more attention to Vern. *If the boy wants to wear himself out that much sooner, then so be it.*

Occasionally, someone would call for a halt, so that they could listen intently for any sounds coming from beyond the wall of rubble. If anyone was alive behind there, the sounds of the rescue effort should have been audible. Any kind of feeble tapping would let the rescuers know that someone was alive and spur them on to greater efforts.

So far, there had been nothing but silence.

Rory turned over his pick to a miner and rested again, speaking briefly to Hannah and downing another cup of scalding black coffee. Then it was back into the mine to take up a shovel and resume digging.

The farther they went now, the more likely it became that the makeshift braces would not hold. Rory Darson was a brave man, but he found himself glancing up at the rough ceiling a foot over his head, knowing how much weight was up there and how easily it would crush out his life if it came tumbling down. All of the men were aware of the danger, and they listened for any telltale rumbles over the clanking and clattering of their tools.

Vern forged ahead of Rory, still pushing himself, his shovel biting into the wall savagely. Rory saw the blood on the handle of Vern's shovel and knew that the deputy's palms were raw meat by now, as hard as he was going at it. He knew that Vern probably would not listen to anything he had to say, but he opened his mouth anyway to try to reason with him.

There was a low rumble above them before Rory could say anything, and suddenly the dust in the air was even thicker. A small chunk of rock bounced off Rory's shoulder, and a man ten feet away screamed.

The knot of men in the tunnel lunged back toward the opening of the shaft, running desperately, some of them dropping their tools. Vern Simmons's head snapped around at the sound of the impending disaster, panic etched on his features. He seemed frozen to the spot where he had stopped digging.

Rory knew in an instant that Vern was not going anywhere on his own. The deputy was too frightened to move. Without thinking about it, Rory reached out with a long arm through the thickening dust and grabbed the collar of Vern's shirt. As more rocks rained around them, Rory threw Vern bodily down the shaft.

"Get out of here!" he yelled, plunging after Vern.

Vern staggered several steps and then caught his balance and tried to pause again. Rory's hand in his back prevented that. Rory shoved him on ahead. The rumbling came again, louder this time.

Rory left his feet in a desperate dive, wrapping his arms around Vern and carrying him along. The men sprawled on the floor of the tunnel, landing heavily on the hard rocky surface. Just behind them, where they had been a second before, a ton of rock came crashing down.

Coughing and blinded, Rory struggled to his feet and lifted Vern. Together, they careened on down the tunnel, boiling out of the mouth of the mine along with the other men fleeing this second cave-in.

The crowd was pressing around the men who had barely escaped being buried alive. Vern slumped to the ground, drawing great, shuddery breaths. Rory stayed on his feet, but just barely. Slowly, he became aware that Odell Winborn was standing next to him, gripping his arm and asking him a question. Rory concentrated and heard the mineowner say, "Was anyone else trapped inside?"

Rory shook his head. "Simmons and I were at the head of the tunnel. We were the last ones out, and I don't think we passed anybody on the way."

"But you can't be sure you didn't miss seeing someone in the confusion?"

Rory's voice was bleak as he answered, "No, I can't be sure."

He glanced over at Vern and saw that Ellen Harwood had appeared out of the crowd. She was on her knees, and Vern's head was pillowed on her ample lap. Tears were running down her face, and as Vern stared up at her like she was some sort of angel, Rory hoped that the deputy was finally seeing what was obvious to everyone else— Ellen Harwood was in love with him.

Hannah called out, "Rory!" He looked up to see her trying to make her way through the mob around him. She was not having much luck. He straightened up and moved to meet her, shouldering between people until she was right in front of him and he could reach out and take her in his arms.

He held her for a long time, knowing how close he had just come to death. To never seeing her again . . .

When he finally became aware that someone was standing next to him, he raised his face from where it was buried in Hannah's hair and saw Vern Simmons, looking truculent as usual. "Thanks for helping me in there, Darson," he said grudgingly. "I could have gotten out all right by myself, though."

Rory did not know whether to laugh or punch the obnoxious man in the face. Both would waste too much

energy, he decided. "No thanks necessary," he said curtly.
"You all right?"

Vern nodded. "I'm fine." He made no mention of his
raw palms, but Rory knew how sore they had to be.

"That's good. Because you know what we've got to do
now."

Hannah spoke up. "Oh, Rory, you're not—"

"Got to," he said. "Let's go dig it out again. There
might still be somebody alive in there."

There were fewer volunteers to go back into the mine
this time, since the second cave-in had proved how unsta-
ble the tunnel now was. But enough men were willing to
risk it that the rescue efforts were able to continue. Finally, just before dawn, they paid off.

Vern Simmons abruptly paused in his digging and cocked
his head to the side. "Wait a minute!" he said urgently.
"Do you hear that?"

Rory had heard it thirty seconds earlier but had said
nothing, unsure whether or not his ears were playing
tricks on him. But now that Vern confirmed it, he nodded.
"I hear it," he said. "It's somebody tapping on the other
side."

The word spread quickly through the tunnel, and men
who had already worked themselves until they were ready
to drop speeded up their efforts to a feverish pace.

Rory's pick and Vern's shovel broke through at the same
time, knocking a small opening into the area of the shaft
that had been sealed off. There was a rush of air from
behind them as life-giving oxygen poured into the stale
atmosphere.

Along with the lingering odor of dust and sweat, Rory
smelled something else when he put his face to the opening: death.

The opening was rapidly enlarged, and several men
climbed through to the other side carrying torches and
canteens of water. Rory was too tired to clamber through
the entrance. He slumped against the wall, the pick dan-

gling limply from his hand. He heard someone crying and
thanking God and knew that there was at least one survivor.

As it turned out, there were two. Both men were in bad
shape from broken bones, dehydration, and lack of good
air. The other six men who had been in the tunnel were
dead.

Rory stayed where he was until the two survivors and
the bodies of the other men had been carried out, and
then he said to the rest of the rescue party, "We'd better
get moving, too. This isn't the safest place in the world."

All of them agreed with that. They made their way back
to the mine entrance, and as they stepped out into the
light of dawn, a cheer went up from the onlookers. The
men were too tired to acknowledge it. They trudged on,
ready to go home and collapse.

Hannah came running up to Rory, and he swept her
into his arms. She clung to him, whispering in his ear,
"Oh, God, Rory, I was so scared! I didn't want to say
anything while you were going back in there, but now that
it's over . . ."

"I know," he murmured. "I know. I was afraid of the
same thing. I was afraid I'd never see you again."

Somewhere along the way, he had fallen in love with
her, and she with him. Either that or he was so tired that
he was imagining things. Whichever was true, he was
going to think about it after he had had some sleep.

As he and Hannah walked back toward her wagon, they
passed Odell Winborn. The mineowner was talking earnestly to Vern Simmons, who was nearly asleep on his
feet. Winborn was saying, "I don't understand what happened. I know the mine was safe. That's why you have to
look into this, Deputy."

Rory did not hear any more. Judging from the way Vern
looked, he was not going to be investigating anything for a
while.

The crowd of people that had hurried to the mine now
trickled away from it, the townspeople returning to their
homes. Rory let Hannah drive the wagon without any
argument this time. To his surprise, he found the wheels
of his mind beginning to turn over as he rode.

"What will this do to the value of Winborn's mine?" he asked.

Hannah glanced at him and frowned. "A cave-in this bad could ruin him," she replied. "It'll cost a lot to dig it out and put the tunnel back in the shape it was. While that's going on, the mine won't be producing much ore, if any. Mr. Winborn may not have enough money to recover."

"So the Vista may wind up virtually worthless."

Hannah nodded. "Easily. Why are you asking questions like that, Rory?"

"Just wondering about a few things," he answered. To tell the truth, he was not sure why it even seemed important to him, but all of his instincts told him it was.

He was also thinking about Vern Simmons's accusation that he had brought trouble with him to Bonanza City. Rory had never believed that a man could be cursed to bring misfortune to others, but it was starting to look as though Vern might have been right. The community had had more than its share of bad luck since he arrived, from Buck Campbell's stabbing to this disaster at the Vista mine.

"Maybe Simmons was right," he said after a moment of silence. "I must have a curse on me, because I sure brought bad luck to town with me."

"I think it's good luck you came when you did," Hannah said quietly. "Otherwise I might never have met you."

Rory grinned. He slipped an arm around her shoulders. He was filthy, but she did not seem to mind.

The wagon rocked on toward town.

Chapter Nine

Rory woke with sunlight slanting into his eyes. He winced and moved his head, and then he rolled over. The bed with its soft mattress and smooth sheets felt wonderful. He stretched luxuriously and then suddenly frowned. This did not feel like his bed back in the boardinghouse.

He sat up abruptly, looking around the room. There was an unfamiliar painting on the wall, sided by a heavy dresser with a mirror and a tall chest of drawers, neither of which he remembered seeing before.

Rory's eyes widened when he saw what was lying on the foot of the bed. It was a small, stuffed doll with braided red hair that reminded him of Hannah.

He knew where he was now. Vaguely, he remembered Hannah driving the wagon back to the Campbell house and insisting that he come inside with her. As worn out as he was, the walk to the boardinghouse was more than he could face. He had allowed himself to be led into the house, taken upstairs, and given the bedroom belonging to one of the girls. Which one of them, he was not sure, but whoever it was had told him that she did not mind doubling up with one of her sisters. Rory had been too tired to argue.

The window in the room faced west, and he could see the sun not far above the mountains. It was late afternoon. He had slept a long time, but considering how hectic the last few days had been, that was no surprise.

Swinging out of bed, he looked down with distaste at

the grime his clothes had left on the sheets. Somebody was going to have to do some washing. He felt bad about that, but he had been much too tired to do anything except take off his gun belt and his boots.

When a soft knock came at the door, Rory turned toward it and called, "Come in."

Hannah opened the door and stuck her head inside the room. "I didn't know if you'd be awake yet or not," she said with a smile.

"Just woke up," Rory said, rolling his shoulders to ease some of the stiffness in them. "That's a mighty fine bed. Sorry I messed up the sheets."

"Don't worry about that. Bess was glad to give it up for the day." Hannah came into the room and saw the doll lying at the foot of the bed. "I see Emily's been here. She said she wanted to bring you one of her dolls so that you'd have some company while you slept. I told her not to disturb you, but I guess she slipped in while none of us were looking."

"She didn't bother me," he said. "Kind of threw me when I woke up and saw it, but other than that . . ."

Hannah looked fresh and rested and beautiful. He did not see how she did it. She could not have slept as much as he had, since she had obviously been up for a while. However she managed it, she was a sight for sore eyes.

"It's sort of late in the day for breakfast, but we've got some food fixed downstairs," Hannah said. "I hope you'll join us."

Rory suddenly realized that he was ravenously hungry. "You bet I will," he declared. "I want to get cleaned up, but I reckon that can wait a little longer."

"By the way," she said, pausing in the doorway, "my father wants to see you as soon as you get a chance."

Rory frowned slightly. "You know what it's about?"

Hannah bit her lip and shook her head. Rory had the feeling that she was not telling the truth. She knew what Buck Campbell wanted to say to him, but for some reason she wanted to keep it to herself.

"How is your pa?" Rory went on when he saw that he was not going to get an answer.

"He's much better. Doctor Madison says that he's going to be fine."

"Glad to hear it. I figured he'd pull through, as tough an old bird as he is."

"He is that," Hannah agreed with a smile.

Rory enjoyed the meal, digging in enthusiastically when Dinah Campbell set a platter of ham, sweet potatoes, and beans in front of him. The food did him as much good as the rest had already done, and by the time Rory was finished he felt human again. His hands were a little sore and raw from the desperate work in the mine tunnel, but not enough to bother him much.

"Your pa still down at the doc's?" Rory asked when the meal was over and he and Hannah had gone out onto the porch.

She nodded. "The doctor didn't want to move him just yet, even though he is improved a lot. Are you going there now?"

Rory shook his head. "I want to get cleaned up. I suppose a fella can get a bath at the barbershop, can't he?"

Hannah blushed prettily at the intimate nature of the question. "I believe so," she said.

"Then I'll go get some clean clothes, take care of that, and then head on over to the doc's." Rory tried to hide the grin that her reaction had provoked.

"I'll meet you over there," Hannah said.

He nodded. For a moment he thought about taking her into his arms and kissing her, but he decided not to when he spotted Emily Campbell peeking at them past a window curtain. Instead, he impulsively made a silly face and winked at the little girl, making her jump back. He heard her giggling inside the house. Then he smiled and nodded to Hannah and started down the street.

As he walked, a sudden realization made his breath catch momentarily in his throat. He had been acting like a kid back there, horsing around with Emily. Until he had come to Bonanza City, he would have sworn that the child inside Rory Darson was long dead, killed by the cold, hard life he had lived.

That life had in some ways been his own choice. Now, he was no longer sure about anything.

He stopped at the boardinghouse long enough to pick up some clean clothes, and then he headed for the barbershop. A tub of hot water cost twenty-five cents, and as Rory stripped and sank into it, he thought it would have been worth ten times that. He soaked for a long time, letting the heat take away the rest of his aches and pains.

He knocked on the door of Dr. Madison's house a little later, dressed in fresh clothes and newly shaven. As the man who had not only captured Sonora Pike but also been a hero of the Vista mine disaster, he discovered that the barber wanted no payment from him. Rory had been prepared to sign an IOU for the man, since he was still out of money, but the barber had waved off the offer. "Reckon you'll find that your money's no good in Bonanza City right now, Mr. Darson," he had said.

Dr. Madison answered his knock after a moment, opening the door and stepping back to let him come inside. "Hello, Mr. Darson," the medical man said. "Miss Campbell said you would be along. She's with her father."

Rory took his hat off and nodded. "Thanks, Doc. I hear you think Buck's going to be all right."

"He's past the critical stage. I'm fairly sure he's going to recover, probably with no permanent damage."

Rory was relieved to hear that. He knew that sheer luck was the only thing that had saved Campbell's life. Nine times out of ten, Pike would have struck a fatal blow in those same circumstances.

The doctor led him to the bedroom and ushered him in. Buck Campbell was sitting up, leaning forward so that the bulky bandage under his nightshirt would not press against the headboard of the bed. His color was much better, and his eyes were alert as he greeted Rory. "Howdy, son," he said, his tone friendlier than Rory had ever heard it.

"Glad to see you, Sheriff." He glanced at Hannah, who was seated beside her father's bed. "I told Hannah you were too ornery to let a little skeeter bite like that keep you down long."

"Skeeter bite, huh?" Campbell snorted. "Pike 'bout carved me like a turkey. I hear you went after that no-good—"

He broke off and glanced at Hannah, then went on, "—*varmint* and brought him back. I'm obliged to you."

"Didn't want that bounty money getting away," Rory said shortly. For some reason, he was uncomfortable with the sheriff's gratitude. He snagged a straight-backed chair, turned it around, and straddled it.

"Uh-huh," Campbell said, sounding as if he did not believe Rory's explanation for a second. It was fine with Rory when he changed the subject by continuing, "Hannah was telling me about the cave-in at the Vista last night. You got any idea what might have caused it?"

Rory shook his head. "I don't know much about mining. I heard that Winborn fella saying that he didn't understand what happened. He claims the mine was perfectly safe, that there was no reason for it to collapse."

Campbell nodded. "Odell Winborn's a smart man, from what I know of him. I'd tend to believe what he was saying when it comes to that mine. Anybody talked to the two men you were able to pull out of there yet?"

The doctor spoke up. "Neither of them is in any shape to be questioned, Sheriff. In fact, they've both been unconscious most of the time."

"Where're they at?"

"They're over at the hotel. I turned one of the rooms into a makeshift hospital, since I didn't have space for them here." Dr. Madison hooked his thumbs in his vest. "There are women watching them, so if there's any change in their condition, I'll know about it right away."

"Sure would like to talk to them boys," Campbell mused. "Could be they could tell us what really happened."

Always the lawman, Rory thought, looking at the bulldog expression on Campbell's face. If he were on his feet, he would not rest until he had dug up all the details of the disaster and its causes.

Campbell shook his head. "Well, there ain't much I can do about it here in this bed, is there?"

"Don't worry about that, Pa. You'll be up and around before you know it," Hannah assured him.

"No, it'll be a while before I'm back to normal." He looked up at Rory. "That's why I've got a favor to ask of you, Darson. Hate to, when you've already done so much for my family, but it don't seem like I've got much choice."

Rory frowned. "What is it, Sheriff?"

Buck Campbell reached over, opened the drawer of a small night table next to the bed, and delved inside it. He extended his hand toward Rory, and on his palm was a battered silver star, the badge of his office. He said, "I want you to wear this for me, until I'm back on my feet."

Rory stared at him. He had never expected anything like this. He glanced over and saw Hannah smiling at him. He had been right; she had known this was coming. After a long moment he replied, "Simmons is your deputy. He figures the job is his while you're on the mend."

Campbell snorted. "Vern ain't really a bad kid, but he ain't sheriff material. Never has been. He can't take care of this town the way it needs to be taken care of. I've got a hunch you can. I've already talked to the mayor, and he and the town council will back me up."

Rory did not know what to say. This vote of confidence by the sheriff had taken him completely by surprise. He reached out and took the badge from Campbell, turned it over in his hands. "You'd ask a bounty hunter to take over for you?"

"My daughter seems to have changed her opinion of bounty hunters, leastways one in particular." Campbell cast a meaningful glance toward Hannah that made her blush. "Reckon I can, too."

Rory took a deep breath and then reached a decision. He pinned the badge to his shirt. As Hannah smiled, he shook hands with Campbell and said, "This is only until you're ready to take over again."

"I understand. But I reckon Vern probably won't."

"You want me to tell him about it?"

Campbell shook his head. "No, I'll send for him. It's my decision, and it's my job to explain it to him. I'd like for him to stay on as your deputy, but I wouldn't count on that."

"I won't." Rory grinned.

"And he's liable to give you trouble. All I ask is that you don't hurt him, Darson. Like I said, he ain't a bad kid."

"Sure, Sheriff. I'll try, but that's all I can promise."

Campbell straightened in the bed and said gruffly, "Now raise your right hand. You got to be sworn in all legal and proper-like."

Rory swore to fulfill his duties as acting sheriff of Saguache County and uphold all the laws of the territory, and then Campbell said, "Reckon your first job's going to be looking into what happened up at the Vista. I ain't so sure it was an accident."

"You think it was sabotage?"

"That's happened more than once in this part of the country. Maybe not in recent years, but I remember a time not long ago when lots of folks wouldn't be above blasting somebody else's claim. Might be a good idea to start asking questions."

Rory agreed and then said, "There's something else I wanted to ask you about, Sheriff. Have you remembered anything else about the night Pike escaped?"

Campbell grimaced. "Hate to say it, but I sure don't, son. Seems like somebody's just whitewashed that part of my memory, because I don't recollect a blamed thing except what I already told you."

Rory was disappointed, but he tried not to show it. He said, "So you still think Pike got out of his cell somehow and clouted you from behind?"

"Don't see how it could've happened any different," Campbell said with a shrug. "Pike's back in jail, so I don't reckon it really matters now."

"I guess not," Rory said slowly. He stood up. "I'll keep you up-to-date on anything I find out about that cave-in."

"That's fine. I know you'll do a good job . . . Sheriff."

That sounded awfully strange to Rory. He said good-bye to Hannah, who was going to sit with her father a little longer, and then caught the doctor's eye as he left the room. Madison followed him out into the parlor.

"I want to ask you a question, Doc," Rory said in a low voice when the bedroom door was closed. "Was there any evidence of a blow to the head when you first examined the sheriff?"

The doctor frowned thoughtfully. "You know, I don't believe there was," he said after a moment. "Of course, at the time I had other things to be concerned about, like that knife wound. But he hasn't exhibited any symptoms of a concussion, which he should have if he had been hit hard enough to knock him out. Trouble is, that old man's head is so hard you might not be able to raise a lump with a fence post. I don't see how that could be important, though."

"It's probably not, Doc. I was just thinking, that's all."

Rory was aware of the curious looks he got from some of the townspeople as he walked from the doctor's house to the sheriff's office. He did not pause to explain why he was wearing the badge, and no one came right out and asked. When he got to the jail and knocked on the door, Luke Warner looked through the peephole and then quickly let him in.

"You living here now, Luke?" Rory asked dryly as he stepped into the office and shut the door behind him.

"No, sir. Vern's been here some. He's pretty busy, though, bein' actin' sheriff and all." Luke squinted at the silver star on Rory's shirt. "Leastways, he was. Does that badge mean what I think it does, Mr. Darson?"

"It does. I just came from talking to Sheriff Campbell. He asked me to take over until he's back on his feet, and I said I would."

A low whistle escaped from the lanky jailer. "Whooeee! Vern ain't gonna like that."

Rory looked intently at him. "What about you? You have any objections to working for me, Luke?"

Luke shook his head. "Not a one."

Rory let a grin crease his face for a moment and then jerked his head toward the cellblock. "Pike giving any trouble?"

"He's been quiet. He eats his meals, sits back there, smokes, and he don't raise a ruckus. He's been guzzling from the bottle you sent. A right good prisoner . . . this time."

"Maybe he'll stay that way until the marshals get here to take him to Denver." Rory saw the weariness in the young man's face and went on, "You're tired, Luke. Go home and get some rest. I'll stay here for a while."

"You sure about that, Sheriff?"

Rory grinned again. "I'm sure. Reckon I'd better get the feel of the place."

Luke accepted the offer gratefully. He put the shotgun that had been cradled in his arms back in the rack on the wall. Rory let him out and relocked the door behind him. Then he spent several minutes looking around the office, discovering where everything was.

There was coffee on the stove, so he poured a cup and carried it over to the door. He opened the peephole and peered through. Night had fallen, and there was not much to see outside.

Rory took a deep breath. The idea of being a lawman, of being responsible for the safety of this town, was still foreign to him. But he had not felt that he could turn down Buck Campbell's request.

He went to the desk, got the keys, and unlocked the cellblock door. Just as Luke Warner had said, Sonora Pike was sitting quietly on his bunk, the tip of his cigarette a glowing red coal in the gathering shadows.

"Howdy, Pike," Rory said.

Pike's head jerked up. He stared at Rory in the light from the office, his eyes narrowing when he spotted the badge on Rory's shirt. "What the hell is all this?" Pike growled.

"I'm the acting sheriff now," Rory replied. "That means I'm responsible for keeping you locked up safe and sound. I just want you to remember that I can always collect that bounty on your corpse."

"You threatenin' me . . . Sheriff?" Pike's tone dripped with sarcasm.

"Just making sure you don't forget how things stand," Rory told him flatly.

"I ain't goin' to forget *anything* about you, bounty man. Now if you're in charge around here, how about seein' to my supper? I'm nigh onto starved."

Rory frowned. He seemed to remember somebody saying that one of the local cafés provided meals for any prisoners in the jail, but he was not sure which one. In any case he could not leave to fetch a meal, not when he was the only one on duty.

The problem was solved for him before he could ponder much longer on it. A knock came on the office door, and when he checked through the peephole, he saw Ellen Harwood standing on the sidewalk, holding a covered tray.

Rory let her in, ready for another expression of surprise that he was taking Campbell's place. Ellen did not seem shocked to see him, however. Hannah had probably talked to her and told her, he thought. But something *was* disturbing her.

"Let me take that tray, ma'am," Rory said. He carried it into the cellblock and passed it through the door to Pike before returning to the office. Ellen was standing beside the desk, looking as though she wanted to say something. He waited for a moment while she gathered up her courage.

Finally, she said, "Hannah told me you were replacing her father for the time being, Mr. Darson. I . . . I'm afraid there might be some trouble."

"With Vern Simmons?" he asked.

Ellen nodded. "He was in my café when Hannah came in and told him that Campbell wanted to see him. After I talked to Hannah, I knew what it was about. I'm just scared of what Vern might do, Mr. Darson. You see, he's awfully hotheaded sometimes."

That was not news to Rory. He smiled and tried to sound reassuring. "I reckon we can work something out. Buck wants Vern to stay on as deputy, and I suppose I do, too."

"But you're not sure?"

"Depends on whether or not he listens to reason."

Ellen smiled wearily. "I'm afraid that's not something Vern is very good at."

The words were barely out of her mouth when a fist pounded heavily on the door. Rory and Ellen looked at each other, and neither was surprised when Vern shouted angrily, "Let me in, Darson!"

Rory sighed. It sounded as if Campbell had had his talk with the deputy. He glanced at Ellen and said quietly, "This has got to be faced sometime."

She nodded. "I know."

Rory came out from behind the desk and went to the door. He thrust the key in the lock and turned it, and no sooner had he done that than Vern shoved the door open and pushed his way into the office, his face red with fury and his hand hovering near the butt of his gun.

"What the hell are you trying to do, Darson?" he demanded.

As Rory slowly shut the door and locked it again, he was considering what to say to this young hellion. "I'm just trying to do what a good man asked me to," he finally replied.

"Buck's hurt and out of his head. He doesn't know what he's doing. Otherwise he'd never have asked bounty-hunting trash like you to pin on a star!"

A muscle in Rory's jaw tightened as he tried to contain his anger. "You're upset, boy," he said in a voice that was little more than a whisper. "You'd best calm down."

Ellen Harwood hurried across the room to Vern's side. He had not seemed to notice her when he came in, but now she clutched his arm urgently. "Please, Vern," she said. "This won't help anything—"

"You'd better get out of here, Ellen," Vern snapped. "This is none of your business."

"But I'm worried about you, Vern."

"Nobody asked you to be," he said harshly.

The hurt look on Ellen's face was almost enough to make Rory give up trying to keep his temper under control. The boy needed to be taken down a notch or two. But for Buck Campbell's sake, Rory decided to try to mend the fences one more time.

"Listen, Vern, Buck and I both want you to stay on as deputy. This is nothing personal against you—"

"The hell it's not! Buck as much as told me he thought I wasn't fit to be sheriff! If that's true, I sure as hell ain't fit to be deputy, either!"

He reached up and ripped the star from his vest, throwing it to the floor at Rory's feet. It bounced off the planks, rolled a couple of feet, and clattered to a stop.

Rory took a deep breath. "If that's the way you want it, that's the way it'll be. Just remember from here on out that you're not a lawman anymore. Step over the line and you'll find yourself back in here on the other side of the bars."

"I'll remember," Vern said tightly. He turned and stalked to the door, then said over his shoulder without looking around, "You want to come and let me out of here, *Sheriff*?"

Without saying anything else, Rory unlocked the door and opened it. Vern strode out, disappearing down the boardwalk.

When Rory turned back to Ellen, he saw that she had picked up Vern's badge. It was in her hands now, and tears were in her eyes. "He . . . he really is a good man. There are just so many things he doesn't understand."

Rory took the badge from her and placed it on the desk. "He'll come around," he said, trying to sound more convinced than he really was. The way he saw it, Vern did not deserve the affections of someone like Ellen Harwood, but he kept those thoughts to himself. Voicing them would just make the young lady feel worse, and anyway, she was not likely to believe him.

She told him that she would pick up the supper tray in the morning, when she brought Pike his breakfast. Rory thanked her and let her out, then stepped out onto the boardwalk himself. He moved a step or two away from the doorway, so that he would not be silhouetted against the light inside, and looked up and down the street.

Bonanza City was its usual busy self tonight. The stores and the saloons were brightly lit and doing a good trade. Folks were going about their own business, not worried about anything except their own concerns.

It had all seemed so simple to him at first. Take Sonora Pike into Bonanza City, wait there for a few days, collect his reward money, and drift on. Now he had a badge on his chest, a former deputy who was angry with him, a killer in his jail . . . and a whole town to take care of.

Chapter Ten

After leaving Odell Winborn the night before, Stefen Kendrick had gone to one of Bonanza City's three houses of ill repute and used some of his carefully hoarded money to purchase the company of a soiled dove named Belinda. Her expertise and a bottle of whiskey had enabled him to forget about Natalie and how she had turned on him. The lovemaking and the liquor had him in such a sated condition that he slept right through the uproar of the mine cave-in.

The next morning he awoke with a pounding headache. Sitting up and blinking his eyes, he looked around at the squalid little room where he had spent the night. Someone stirred beside him under the sheets. He glanced over and saw the tousled blond hair and heavily painted face of a whore who could not have been more than sixteen.

Kendrick closed his eyes for a moment and shook his head, trying to clear away some of the cobwebs. Sunlight was coming in through the window. That meant he had spent the night and, more importantly, spent more money than he should have. He touched the wound on his cheek. It was Natalie's fault that he was even here in this brothel. He should have been back in the hotel with her.

He slipped out of bed, being careful not to wake the girl. *Belinda*, that was her name, he remembered foggily. With the splitting headache and the awful taste in his mouth, he did not feel like making idle conversation with a whore. He got dressed as quickly as possible.

The house was quiet at this early hour. He went down a hall to the stairs and descended to the parlor with its traditional gilt and red-velvet appointments. His hand was on the doorknob when a hoarse voice rasped behind him, "Good morning, sir."

Kendrick looked over his shoulder and saw the madam standing in a doorway, a silk robe wrapped loosely around her blowsy figure. There was a glass of whiskey in her hand. Uneasily, he said, "Good morning."

"Belinda treat you nice, did she?"

"Just fine," he assured her. "She's a wonderful girl."

"She's a slut," the madam said dryly. "But she's good at it. Sorry about all the ruckus last night."

Kendrick frowned. "Ruckus? I didn't hear anything." The sudden fear struck him that the authorities might have raided the place; he did not want Winborn to know that he patronized such an establishment. But no, if that had happened, he would surely have been awakened.

"There was a cave-in up at one of the mines," the madam said. "Just about the whole town turned out to help." She laughed harshly. "Some of the girls got a little upset when their customers jumped up and ran out right in the middle of things. You know how these miners are, though."

A feeling of disaster overwhelmed Kendrick's senses, and he gripped the doorsill for support as he asked, "Which mine was it?"

"The Vista. Odell Winborn's claim. From what I hear, it's just about ruined."

The room seemed to spin around Kendrick. He felt as if the floor was going to fall out from under him. Swallowing, he licked his lips, and he could feel beads of sweat spring out on his face.

"Say, mister, you don't look so good," the madam said, frowning. "You need a drink?"

He managed to shake his head. "N-no. Thanks anyway. I . . . I've got to be going."

"Sure. I could use some sleep myself. It was a long night." She grinned. "Ain't they all?

Kendrick got out the door somehow and staggered away

from the place. He found himself on the boardwalk, heading toward the hotel.

The Vista was ruined! All his plans, all his work, for nothing! He could hardly believe the news, but as he passed by small groups of townspeople, he heard them talking about the catastrophe. Evidently several men had died in the accident, and the damage to the mine was enormous.

Accident? Kendrick abruptly remembered the threat Natalie had hissed at him the night before. She had vowed that the mine he wanted so badly would be worthless . . . and now it was.

He stopped and took a deep breath. It was ludicrous even to think such a thing. There was no way Natalie could have called down some sort of curse to cause this disaster.

He would go see her, talk to her, reason with her. She was probably over her anger by now, and he could make her see that it was time for them to move on and start over somewhere else. There were plenty of other wealthy men in the world who could be blinded by a pretty face and a lush body. The two of them had to put this debacle behind them.

Kendrick started toward the hotel again, his steps quicker and more purposeful.

Natalie was at the dresser in her room, brushing her thick dark hair, when the knock came on the door. A slight smile played over her features. She recognized the knock. He had come crawling back, as she had known he would. He was going to be surprised when he found out how different things were going to be in the future.

"Come in, Stefan," she called softly.

He stepped into the room and closed the door behind him. She could tell from the expression on his face that something had shocked him, and she guessed that he had heard the news about Winborn's mine.

"Something awful has happened, Natalie," he said as she continued brushing her hair.

"I know," she replied. "I told you it would, Stefan."
Her tone was casual and unconcerned.

"You can't mean that you caused that cave-in. Why,
that's—"

"Don't say it," she warned him. "You've said quite
enough about my powers recently, Stefan."

He passed a hand over his sweating face. "All right," he
said slowly. "We won't say anything more about that. The
important thing is that we work well together, Natalie. I
think we should move on and find another mark."

Natalie put her brush down and turned to face him.
"No, Stefan," she said, shaking her head. "I'm not ready
to leave Bonanza City yet."

He lifted his hands in frustration. "But there's no reason
for us to stay. Winborn may be able to salvage his operation, given enough time and money, but that won't do us
any good."

"I have my reasons." She said no more. Let him wonder
what her reasons were. She was not going to tell him that
she could not leave while her brother was in jail and that
bounty hunter was still alive and unpunished.

He stepped closer to her, and some of the threatening
edge was back in his voice as he spoke. "I say we leave."

Natalie smiled at him, taking him by surprise. "And I
say we stay," she replied as she moved closer to him. She
lifted her fingers to the wound on his face, touched it
caressingly. Anger flared in Kendrick's eyes, but it was
replaced by lust as she molded her body to his. Her lips
found his mouth while her hands strayed down his body.

The spell of bewitchment she had cast earlier was working perfectly, she thought. She entranced him with lips
and tongue and fingers, and when she was done with him,
he was unable to put up any more arguments. He agreed
that they should stay on in town for another day or two.

The pendulum had swung. Natalie knew, to her deep
satisfaction, that she was now in charge. And she intended
never to let go of that power.

They stayed in her room most of the day, Natalie draining him, strengthening her hold on him. By the time the
shadows of dusk began to gather, she knew that Kendrick

would do anything she asked of him, bound by his own lust and the spell she had woven.

She had complete confidence in her powers now, but if they occasionally needed assistance—as had been the case the night before—she was perfectly capable of that as well.

She left him lying in her bed and began to dress.

"Where are you going?" he asked sleepily.

"I need a few things from the store," she told him. Actually, what she needed more than anything else was a breath of fresh air. The day had been long and tedious for her, no matter how much he had enjoyed it. But it was work that needed doing. "Why don't I meet you down in the restaurant for dinner in half an hour or so?"

"All right," Kendrick said. "Maybe I'll nap a little more."

"That's fine, Stefan." Natalie's voice was soft and silky, and the sound of it made him smile as he closed his eyes.

Kendrick did not see the look on her face as she slipped out of the room. *He is a fool*, she thought, *but from now on he will be a useful fool*.

Night had fallen by the time she left Thaddeus Montrose's general store with several small packages in her hands. Her eyes were drawn across the street to the sheriff's office. The awareness that her brother was locked up in there again was like a knife in her belly. She had to get him out and see him safely away before she could leave here, and she had to move quickly, since the marshals from Denver would probably be here within another day or two.

Suddenly the door of the sheriff's office opened, and a man came stalking out. Natalie recognized him as Vern Simmons, the young deputy who had taken over as acting sheriff. Her eyes narrowed as she saw in the light from one of the streetlamps that he no longer wore his badge. Perhaps he had been stripped of his office for some reason. He certainly looked upset about something.

Instinct told her to follow him. Moving quickly, she angled across the street and managed to reach the board-walk just a few feet behind him. He was walking at a fast pace, and she might not have been able to catch up to him if he had not suddenly stopped, leaned on a post, and sighed heavily.

Natalie immediately smiled at him. "Why, hello, Sheriff," she said sweetly.

Vern Simmons glanced sharply at her, his features tight with anger, but he caught himself before uttering what was obviously going to be a hot reply. He paused and then said, "Evening, ma'am." He did not seem to remember her.

"It's certainly a pretty night, isn't it?"

He made a bitter sound in his throat. "I'm not so sure about that."

"Is something the matter, Sheriff? You seem rather disturbed."

"Damn right I am!" He shook his head. "Pardon me, ma'am. It's just that I'm not the sheriff anymore. Campbell's appointed somebody else to take his place for the time being."

Natalie made her voice sincere as she said, "I'm sorry to hear that. Who did he appoint?"

"That blamed, no-good bounty hunter! Darson!"

Natalie's breath caught in her throat, and she felt an icy finger trail along her spine. So Rory Darson was now the sheriff! That was a development she had not expected. Slowly, a smile spread across her face. This did not have to be such a bad turn of fate if she played her hand right.

"I remember Mr. Darson," she said. "I came into town on the same stage with him and his prisoner."

Vern nodded. "I thought you looked familiar, ma'am. You'd be Miss Ingram." He seemed to have calmed down somewhat during his conversation with her.

"That's right. And I thought Mr. Darson was absolutely brutal to his prisoner during the stage trip! I'm shocked the sheriff wanted him to act in his place."

"You and me both, ma'am."

She looked shyly at him and went on, "I was just on my way back to the hotel, Mr. Simmons. Would you be so kind as to accompany me? I realize a lady is perfectly safe on the streets of your city, but I would still appreciate the company."

"Sure thing, ma'am." He took her arm. "I don't know how much longer the streets are going to be safe, not with a man like Darson in charge."

"Well, perhaps Sheriff Campbell will see the error of his ways and reappoint you," she said encouragingly.

"Don't think I'd take the job now," Vern said gruffly. "Not after the way I've been treated." He reached across his body for the packages she was carrying. "Let me help you with those, ma'am."

"Why, thank you, Mr. Simmons."

"Call me Vern, why don't you?"

Her smile widened. "I'd be glad to . . . Vern."

It was almost too easy, she thought. He was almost as easy to manipulate as Kendrick had proven to be—and she had not even had to take off her clothes.

As they strolled along the boardwalk toward the hotel, her brain was working feverishly behind the smiling mask she wore. Already she saw a way to take advantage of Rory Darson's new position as sheriff. Not only would she have her revenge on him, but her brother would be free once again.

And this time, Rory Darson would die before he had the chance to go after Sonora Pike.

Luke Warner returned to the jail sooner than Rory had expected. "I got to thinkin' you might need me to watch the place while you got some supper, Sheriff," Luke said after Rory had let him in. "I already ate."

"Thanks, Luke," Rory told him. "I had a big meal late this afternoon, but if you don't mind staying here for a while, there is one errand I need to take care of."

"Sure thing, Mr. Darson." Luke glanced at the cell-block door. "Reckon I'm gettin' used to havin' Pike back there. He don't spook me none anymore."

Rory tried not to grin. Luke's words were brave, but he could still see the nervousness in the deputy's eyes. A little edginess was not such a bad thing; it would keep Luke on his toes.

Rory found out from the deputy which of the big houses

on the edge of town belonged to Odell Winborn and headed there after he was sure that Luke had locked the door behind him. There was a chance that Winborn would be up at his mine, but Rory doubted it. The mineowner could not accomplish much up there at night.

Lights were burning in Winborn's mansion. It was set back from the street slightly, a forbidding two-story structure topped with a steep roof. A wrought-iron fence surrounded the yard. Rory entered through an ornate gate and then went up onto the porch. Next to the door was a bell cord that set off a deep, peeling note somewhere inside when he tugged it.

Odell Winborn opened the door himself a moment later. In the light from the foyer, his face was haggard, weariness etching deep lines in his features. His eyes were dull, but a slight spark of interest lit in them when he saw the badge on Rory's chest.

"Good evening, Mr. Darson," he said solemnly.

Rory nodded. "Mr. Winborn. Reckon I could talk to you for a few minutes?"

"Is this an . . . official request?"

"Yes, sir. Buck Campbell appointed me the acting sheriff earlier this evening."

Winborn stepped back to let Rory into the house. "By all means. Come in, Mr. Darson. How can I help you?"

He led Rory into a darkly paneled study and sat down behind a big desk, gesturing for Rory to take the armchair in front of it. Rory took his hat off and sat down, feeling uncomfortable in the plush chair. Holding his hat between his knees, he leaned forward and said, "I guess you know what I'm here to talk about."

"The cave-in." Winborn nodded. "I would have expected some sort of official investigation if someone other than Vern Simmons had been in charge. I didn't believe he had enough initiative to start one."

"It was Buck's idea. He wants me to nose around some, and I figured you'd be the best place to start."

Winborn leaned back in his chair and took a cigar from a humidor on the desk. He did not light it, just toyed with it in his fingers. "I'll be more than happy to tell you anything I can, Sheriff."

"You and your men have had a day to dig around up there. Did you find anything to indicate what caused the cave-in?"

Winborn shook his head. "No. We found nothing. But I would bet my life that shaft was safe, Mr. Darson. I was a hard-rock miner myself once, you know." He waved toward a daguerreotype on the wall behind him. The print showed a group of miners posing in front of an open shaft. "That was made twenty years ago in California, when I was swinging a pick and shovel." He straightened, and his voice became more intense as he went on. "I inspected the mine at least once a week, Mr. Darson. I know the support timbers were well placed and in good condition. I have no explanation for the shaft's collapsing."

"Have you considered sabotage?" Rory asked quietly.

With a grimace Winborn said, "Of course. But I don't believe that to be the case. There was a time when a mineowner might not hesitate to blow up a competitor's tunnel, but those days are in the past. We're respectable businessmen now; we've driven the criminals out. Besides, the men who own the other mines in the area are friends of mine. They wouldn't do such a thing."

Rory did not doubt the sincerity of Winborn's statements, but there was always the chance that he had misjudged his competitors. Nevertheless, his instincts told him that Winborn was right.

The mineowner sighed and shook his head. "This is a terrible thing. Losing those men like that . . . I take the responsibility, Sheriff. I will provide for their families, and for the families of the injured men." He stuck the cigar in his mouth and said around it, "I had such hopes for the Vista."

"I thought it had already done real well for you," Rory said.

"Oh, it had. But I was planning to make improvements and make it an even better claim. I was about to hire a new manager, and between us I'm sure we could have built the Vista up to the same level as the Exchequer or the Bonanza. Now the shaft has been weakened so much that it will probably have to be abandoned. I've told my men that they're free to look for other work."

"You said something about a new manager?" Rory asked, something prodding him to hang onto this thread.

"Yes. I was going to hire Mr. Stefan Kendrick. You may know him. I believe he and his cousin came into town on the same stage as you did."

Rory frowned. He remembered Kendrick, all right, and he remembered the woman who had been traveling with him. They had given the impression they were lovers rather than relatives. But perhaps more importantly, Rory had come away from that stagecoach ride with the feeling that Kendrick knew precious little about mining.

So why would a man with Winborn's experience and business savvy hire somebody like Kendrick to manage his mine?

But Rory said nothing about that question. Instead, he thanked Winborn for his cooperation and stood up to leave. "I'll let you know if I find out anything," he promised.

"I'd appreciate that, Sheriff." Winborn sighed again. "You can't imagine how devastating this whole affair has been."

"No, sir. But I'll get to the bottom of it if I can."

Rory considered what he had learned as he walked down the street toward the jail. The connection between Winborn, Kendrick, and the woman—he suddenly remembered that her name was Natalie Ingram—was an intriguing one. Could Kendrick have had something to do with the cave-in? That did not seem likely, since Winborn was going to hire him to manage the mine.

When Luke Warner let him into the sheriff's office, Rory saw that they had a visitor. A short, rotund man, bald except for a fringe of white hair around his ears, was standing beside the desk.

"Mr. Montrose here wants to talk to you, Sheriff," Luke said as he relocked the door.

"Thaddeus Montrose, sir," the man said, extending his hand to Rory. "I own the General Mercantile establishment down the street."

Rory nodded. "I've seen your place, Mr. Montrose," he said as he shook the man's hand. "What can I do for you?"

"I'm here to report a robbery, Sheriff."

"Your store was held up?"

Montrose pointed to a bump on his bald head. "Somebody clouted me from behind and knocked me out, Sheriff."

"When did this happen?"

"Last night."

Rory frowned. "Last night?" he asked, surprised. "How come you didn't report it then?"

"Well, everyone was gone last night during all that uproar about the mine cave-in, and today I was just too busy at the store to get away until closing time."

Rory sat down behind the desk, wishing that the merchant had reported the crime earlier. It was going to be hard to pick up any kind of a trail after nearly twenty-four hours. "What did the robbers take?"

"They stole some dynamite from my storeroom. That's all I could find missing. I keep plenty on hand, what with all the mining in the area, you know. I suppose I'm lucky they didn't clean me out."

"Reckon so," Rory grunted. "You didn't get a look at whoever hit you?"

"None at all. In fact, I thought I was alone in the store when the crime occurred."

Rory glanced at Luke. "You feel up to staying here a little longer?"

"I'm fine, Sheriff," Luke assured him. "You just go ahead and do whatever you think's best."

Rory stood up again. "We'll go over to your store, Mr. Montrose, and take a look around. Maybe if we can find where the culprit got in, that'll tell us something." He did not hold out much hope of being able to locate the robber or robbers, but he was the sheriff now, and he had to make an effort to solve the crime.

The two men went to the general store, with Montrose hurrying to keep up with Rory's long strides. Rory examined the lock on the front door, checked the windows, and took a look at the back door. Nowhere was there any sign of a forced entry.

Montrose scratched his head. "They had to get in some-how. I've got the lump on my noggin to prove it."

"Were you still open for business when all this hap-pened?"

"The front door was open," Montrose nodded. "The back door and all the windows were locked, though."

A possibility occurred to Rory. "You reckon one of your customers could've hidden somewhere in the store until you were alone, then jumped you?"

"I guess that could have happened," Montrose said dubiously. "But I certainly don't think so. Why, the only customer I had for a couple of hours beforehand was a woman, and I hardly think—"

"Did you know her?" Rory cut in.

"Yes, indeed. A very lovely young woman. She was in again today, in fact, earlier. It was Miss Ingram, from over at the hotel."

Rory stiffened. "Natalie Ingram?"

"I believe that is her name. Dark hair, very, ah, exotic looking . . ."

That was Natalie Ingram, all right. Rory rubbed his jaw in thought. He was beginning to see some sort of pattern here. But pattern or not, he could not make sense of it all just yet.

Montrose was frowning at him. "Sheriff," he said, "you can't believe that Miss Ingram had anything to do with what happened to me."

"We'll see, Mr. Montrose." Rory left the store abruptly, heading toward the doctor's house. A sense of urgency gripped him.

Dr. Madison answered his knock in shirt sleeves, his tie off. The doctor smiled and said, "Good evening, Mr. Darson. Are you here to see Sheriff Campbell again? It's rather late, you know."

Rory shook his head, pitching his voice low as he an-swered, "I'd rather Buck didn't know anything about this yet, Doc, since nothing may come of it."

Madison looked puzzled. "Come of what, Mr. Darson?"

"Has there been any improvement in either of those miners over at the hotel?"

"As a matter of fact, I've just come from there a few minutes ago. One of the men regained consciousness. I think he's going to be all right."

"I've got to talk to him, Doc," Rory said. When Madison began to look doubtful, Rory went on, "It's important. I may have a lead on what caused the cave-in."

"Well . . . I'm not sure he should be disturbed, but I suppose we can risk a minute or so. You'll have to call a halt when I say so, though."

Rory nodded. "Agreed."

"Just let me get my coat."

Rory could tell that the doctor was curious as they walked toward the hotel, but he did not offer to explain the theory he was developing. There was still too much that he did not know.

The two injured miners were in a room at the rear of the ground floor in the hotel. The clerk greeted Rory and Madison by saying, "Howdy, Doc. You back again so soon?"

The doctor inclined his head toward Rory. "Sheriff Darson here needs to talk to Gehringer if he's still awake."

"*Sheriff* Darson? But I thought—" The clerk broke off and grinned uneasily. "Sorry, Sheriff. I didn't see the badge at first. I thought Vern Simmons was the acting sheriff."

"He was," Rory said shortly. "Buck Campbell asked me to take over."

"That's true," the doctor confirmed. "Come on, Sheriff. I'll see if the miner can talk."

Rory waited outside the room as Madison went in. After a moment the doctor opened the door and motioned for him to enter. There were two narrow beds in the room. The man in the one next to the window was heavily bandaged, both arms and one leg in splints. His eyes were closed, and his breath rasped as he slept. The other man was awake and relatively alert. His midsection was wrapped in bandages, as was the side of his head.

"Howdy . . . Sheriff," he said weakly. "Doc says you want . . . to talk to me."

Madison stepped to the bedside, where a woman sat in

a chair. "We'll be all right, Mrs. Bowden," he told her. "Why don't you take a break?"

When the volunteer nurse was gone, the doctor continued, "Sheriff, this is Walt Gehringer. He's still very weak, so please keep your questions short."

Rory nodded. He sat down in the chair and leaned close to the injured man. "Glad to see you're getting better, Gehringer," he said. "Reckon you can tell me what happened up there at the Vista last night?"

The miner took a deep breath, wincing at the pain from what were probably broken ribs. "The . . . the whole shebang come down around our heads," he said. "We were workin' one second . . . and then there was a blast."

"Like a dynamite blast?" Rory's question was quick.

Walt Gehringer managed a nod. "Could've been. Hard to say. . . . There was so much noise right afterwards. . . ."

The doctor knelt beside Rory's chair. "You think it was sabotage, Sheriff?"

Rory nodded. Keeping his attention on Gehringer, he asked, "Did you see anybody unusual around the mine before the explosion?" His pulse began to pound faster as he posed the question. Just the fact that an explosion caused the cave-in was confirmation of part of his theory. The miner's answer could wrap up the rest of it.

But the man shook his head after a long moment. "Didn't . . . didn't see nobody who wasn't supposed to be there. Reckon somebody could've . . . slipped into the shaft. Weren't no guards there. No need for 'em."

Gehringer's eyes closed, and the doctor put a hand on Rory's arm. "That's enough," he whispered. "We'd better let him sleep now."

Rory stood up and slipped out of the room behind the doctor. He was confused. He was glad that he had confirmed the suspicions that he and Campbell both held about sabotage, but he wished the miner had seen the person who had planted the dynamite. It would have been nice to have some proof, even though Rory thought he knew who the culprit was.

The way he saw it, Stefan Kendrick had caused the Vista cave-in.

He had no idea why Kendrick would have done such a thing, especially when he was about to begin working at the mine. But Rory was fairly sure now that Natalie Ingram was the one who had knocked out old Thaddeus Montrose and stolen the dynamite from his storeroom. He could not imagine Natalie skulking around the mine and planting explosives in the shaft, so he figured that Kendrick had handled that part of the job. There was only one way to find out why they had done it. Direct action was what Rory knew best; Kendrick and Natalie would talk when he arrested them and threw them in jail.

He thanked the doctor for letting him talk to the injured miner and then went to the lobby to get the numbers of Kendrick's and Natalie's rooms. He had just been told the room numbers by the puzzled clerk and had started toward the stairs when the front door banged open. Rory turned that way, his hand instinctively going to the gun on his hip, and saw Vern Simmons stalk into the lobby, his face stormy.

Vern came to an abrupt halt when he spotted Rory. He said, "All right, Darson! It's time you and me had it out!"

Rory could smell the whiskey on the young man's breath. Vern had probably been drinking ever since leaving the sheriff's office earlier. "You'd better ease off, Vern," Rory said quietly. "You're about to get into more than you can handle."

"I can handle you, bounty hunter," Vern sneered. "Saw you through the window and told myself it was time somebody put you in your place. I'm just the man to do it, mister."

Rory glanced at the stairs. According to the clerk, Kendrick and Natalie were up there—and if Rory's theory was right, they had the answers to a lot of questions. He did not want to hurt Vern Simmons, but he did not have much time to waste on him, either.

Buck Campbell had believed that there was a decent lawman somewhere inside Vern's immaturity. Rory decided he would make one last attempt to cut through it. "Listen, Vern," he said urgently, trying to penetrate the liquor haze in the young man's brain. "I'm on the track of the people who caused the cave-in up at the Vista mine. Now follow me on this and see what you think. . . ."

As she stepped from her room into the upstairs hall, Natalie Ingram heard a voice that she recognized. It belonged to that bounty hunter, Rory Darson; he was down in the lobby right now. Staying away from the landing, out of sight from below, she moved close enough to make out his words.

Her blood seemed to turn to ice water as she heard him detailing his suspicions to that dim-witted deputy. He was remarkably accurate in his speculations, with one major exception—it was *she* who had planted the dynamite in the mine shaft and set off the explosion. Kendrick had known nothing about it. Natalie was not surprised that the bounty hunter suspected Kendrick of being behind it all. Most men saw her beauty and little else. They took no notice of the brain behind her features, knew nothing of the fires that burned within her.

If Rory Darson ever got his hands on them, she thought, Kendrick would collapse. Natalie was sure of that. He would plead innocence, would point the finger of guilt at her just to save his own skin, even though he had no idea she really was to blame for the blast at the mine.

Natalie's lips drew back from her teeth in an ugly smile. She had wanted to move quickly on her new plan. Now she had no choice.

She went to the door of Kendrick's room, where he had gone earlier to dress for dinner. Without knocking, she opened it and slipped in.

He was working with his tie, trying to get the knot right, when he looked into the mirror and saw her tensely standing there just inside the door. "What's wrong, Natalie?" he asked quickly.

"You said we should leave, Stefan. I think you were right."

He frowned. "But you said—"

"Never mind what I said! We have to go, and we have to go now."

There had been a time when he would have argued with her, but now, with the shift in their relationship, he shrugged and nodded. "I think it's awfully sudden, but if it's what you want . . ."

"It is." She bent and pulled his valise from under the bed. "Start packing. Quickly."

Vern Simmons stared owlishly at Rory as he listened to what the new acting sheriff had to say. When Rory was finished explaining his theory, Vern hesitated a moment and then snorted derisively. "That's the wildest bunch of nonsense I've ever heard!" he said. "You haven't got the least bit of proof. Anyway, that Miss Ingram is a nice lady. She wouldn't be mixed up in anything crooked."

Rory shook his head. "I don't have time to argue with you, Vern. We'll just have to settle our differences later." He stepped forward, shouldering his way past the angry former deputy.

"Hold on, you son of a bitch!" Vern lashed out, grabbing Rory's arm.

With that, Rory's temper exploded. He whirled around, whipping his free arm across in a backhand that cracked into Vern's jaw. Vern lost his hold on Rory's arm and staggered back, catching his balance against an armchair before he fell. By the time he straightened up, Rory had climbed half the staircase.

Rory was close enough to the landing to see the door opening in the hall. Kendrick and Natalie came out of her room, each of them carrying a bag, and suddenly Rory realized that they were running out. Somehow, they must have found out that he suspected them.

His hand dropped to his gun. "You two stop right there!" he called. "You're under arrest!"

He heard Vern Simmons charging up the stairs behind him, but he ignored the young hothead. There was no time to mess with Vern now, because Rory saw Kendrick's hand diving under his coat. He knew it would come out with a gun.

Rory drew his Colt smoothly, but Kendrick was a fraction faster. The small revolver in the man's hand cracked, and Rory felt the slug whip by his head. He heard it thud into something behind him, and then he heard Vern's sudden gasp of pain. Rory squeezed off a shot, but just as he fired, Vern slumped into him from behind, throwing his aim off and sending the bullet into the wall beyond Kendrick and Natalie.

Vern was babbling in pain and clutching at him as Kendrick and Natalie spun around and raced toward the rear stairs. Rory tried to disentangle himself, but he was too late. Vern was bleeding heavily, and Rory's boot slipped in the blood that was splashed on the stairs. He caught himself and muttered curses as the running footsteps faded.

Vern was going to bleed to death if no one tended to his wound in a hurry. Rory holstered his gun and knelt to support the young man who was sprawled on the stairs. Kendrick's bullet had taken him high in the chest, tearing through muscle and shattering bone. Rory jerked his neckerchief off and jammed it into the wound. When he saw the frightened clerk stick his head up over the desk, he snapped, "Go get the doc! The shooting's over; it's safe enough."

Looking doubtful of that, the clerk ran out from behind the desk and hurried to the front door, slamming it behind him and running down the street, yelling for the doctor at the top of his lungs.

Rory stayed where he was, holding Vern Simmons. Vern was shaking, and as Rory watched, his eyes rolled up in his head as he passed out from the pain.

That bullet was meant for me, Rory thought, and once again he found himself wondering if Vern had been right all along. Maybe he had brought all this trouble to Bonanza City.

Chapter Eleven

Hannah and Emily Campbell were alone in the big front room of their house. The other girls had already gone to bed, and Emily should have been there, too, but she seemed to be coming down with a slight cold. Hannah was willing to spoil her, for a little while at least.

They were sitting together in a big chair, Emily snuggled close to Hannah as the older sister read from a battered storybook that had been passed down from one daughter to the next. Emily listened intently while Hannah finished the story. Then she looked up and said, "Could we read one of Pa's Deadwood Dick stories next, Hannah? They're more fun."

Hannah tried not to smile. "Little girls don't read such things, Emily."

"Why not?"

"Well . . . they're for grown-ups. All those stories about Indians and outlaws might give you bad dreams."

Emily protested, "But there's Injuns and outlaws around here anyway, and I don't have bad dreams."

The little girl had a point, Hannah thought, but there were still certain proprieties to observe. "Maybe another time," she said gently.

Changing the subject abruptly, as children will, Emily said, "You like Rory, don't you, Hannah?"

The question took Hannah by surprise. After a moment, she said, "Yes, I think I do. I like him very much."

"Are you going to marry him?"

Hannah did not answer. She was lost in thought. If the truth were told, she was probably in love with Rory Darson. He had lived a hard existence, but she suspected that under his tough exterior was a man who was simply afraid of being hurt too badly again. His sister had died in his arms, and he had seen the rest of his family slaughtered. The near death of Buck Campbell had been enough to help Hannah understand how such a tragedy could shape the rest of a person's life. But with time—and love—things could change for Rory. She knew they could.

Emily pulled on her sleeve. "You didn't answer me," she accused. "Are you going to marry Rory or not?"

"He hasn't asked me," Hannah said.

"But if he does?"

Hannah smiled. "We'll just have to wait and see, I guess."

"That's no answer," Emily pouted. "I'd surely marry him if he asked me. I'd marry him in a minute."

"I wouldn't tell him that," Hannah advised solemnly. "You might scare him off."

A sudden knock on the door forestalled anything else Emily had to say and made both of them look up. "Maybe that's him!" Emily exclaimed.

Hannah stood up. She was not expecting Rory back tonight, now that he had the duties of sheriff to perform, but perhaps he was taking a break, she reasoned, leaving Luke Warner in charge at the jail. She went to the door, Emily trailing closely behind her, turned the knob, and opened it.

The smile on her face vanished as two people suddenly pushed into the house from the porch. Hannah recognized them from the stagecoach as Natalie Ingram and Stefan Kendrick—but what did they want here?

Kendrick's hand came up, and Hannah saw with a shock that he held a gun. She only had time to say, "What—" before Kendrick gestured sharply with the weapon.

"Shut up!" he barked. "You and the little girl keep still, lady."

Natalie smoothly shut the door behind her and then

faced the stunned woman. In a low voice she asked Hannah, "Where are the others?"

Hannah swallowed. She could see the hatred and the menace in the older woman's eyes, although she did not understand the reasons for them. She said, "My sisters have gone to bed. What do you want?"

"Call them out here," Natalie commanded.

For a moment, Hannah considered instead calling to the other girls and telling them to run for help. But Emily was standing close beside her, clutching her long skirt. She could not take a chance on angering Kendrick, not while he was holding that pistol.

"Bess! Dinah! Melanie!" she raised her voice. "Come in here, please." When there was no response, she yelled, "*Girls!* Come out here! Now!"

The girls trooped in from their rooms a moment later, wearing nightgowns and rubbing sleep from their eyes. They stopped in their tracks when they saw the two strangers.

Kendrick moved the gun slightly so that its barrel covered all of them. As Hannah looked at him, she thought she saw confusion on his face, as though he was unsure of what he was doing here. Not so Natalie, however; she was undoubtedly in charge now.

Natalie stepped closer to Hannah and peered into her eyes. The two women were about the same height. Hannah met the other woman's gaze and tried not to show how worried she was, although she thought that Natalie looked more than a little touched in the head. Quietly, Hannah said, "What do you want?"

"*Revenge,*" Natalie hissed with a smile. "Something you wouldn't understand, you insipid little fool. Rory Darson is going to feel pain, the same way that I have felt pain."

At the mention of her hero's name, Emily gathered her courage. "You leave Rory alone," she warned in quavering tones.

Hannah put her hand on Emily's shoulder and squeezed gently. "Hush, now," she said. "No one's going to hurt Rory."

"That's where you're wrong, bitch," Natalie spat.

Kendrick's confusion finally forced him to speak. "Natalie, what is this?" he demanded. "Why did you drag me here? We've got to get out of town!" Despite his questions, the barrel of his gun did not waver.

Natalie shook her head. "Not yet. Not until we have what we need."

She put a hand on Hannah's chest and gave her a sudden shove backward. Hannah cried out and caught her balance, but not before Natalie's fingers swooped down and cruelly gripped Emily's arm. The dark-haired woman jerked the little girl toward her and said, "You're coming with me, brat!"

"No!" Hannah cried. She knew now what they wanted—they were going to kidnap Emily! She lunged forward, ignoring the threat of Kendrick's gun.

Natalie met the attack with a sharp backhanded slap, which Hannah could not avoid. As the other girls started forward, Kendrick ducked to the side so that he could cover them better. "Hold it!" he snapped. Bess, Dinah, and Melanie had no choice but to do as he said.

Natalie thrust the squirming, terrified Emily toward Kendrick. With his free hand, he gripped the girl's arm and twisted hard, making her cry out and stop struggling.

Shaking her head to clear away the effects of Natalie's blow, Hannah narrowed her eyes and regarded the older woman. "I won't let you do it," she said.

"Stop me then," Natalie dared.

The redheaded woman leaped at Natalie again. Hannah was no fighter, but she had been involved in the usual amount of rough-and-tumble with her sisters as they were growing up. She went after Natalie's eyes with one hand and tried to tangle the fingers of her other hand in the long dark hair of her enemy.

Natalie dodged to the side, bringing up a fist that cracked into Hannah's jaw. Hannah staggered, but she managed to get hold of Natalie's dress, and she pulled Natalie along with her.

The women tripped and fell, landing heavily on the floor. Hannah heard Emily sobbing, but there was no time to do anything except try to defend herself. Natalie fought with a strange smile on her face, gouging at Hannah's eyes, driving her fists into the redheaded woman's middle, and clawing at her breasts. Using her fists with the intention to hurt was foreign to Hannah, but in desperation she doubled her hands and launched wild punches at Natalie's head.

One of the blows caught Natalie in the eye and knocked her off her opponent. Hannah rolled and dove after her, trying to make use of the momentary advantage.

Natalie's knee came up, smashing into Hannah's stomach. Groaning, Hannah fell to the side, but Natalie fell on top of her, landing with her elbows jabbing savagely into Hannah's bosom. Hannah could not get her breath, and the pain in her body was throwing a reddish haze over her eyes. She pushed at Natalie as the older woman's fingers hooked around her throat. The red mist began to turn black. . . .

"Come on! Come on, dammit! You're killing her!"

Vaguely, Hannah was aware of Kendrick's low-pitched but urgent pleas. They must have gotten through to Natalie as well, because the pressure on Hannah's throat suddenly eased. Natalie released her hold and climbed to her feet, looking down triumphantly at her defeated opponent. Natalie's dress was torn and gaped open in several places, exposing black lace and white skin, but she did not seem to care.

Taking a deep breath, Natalie said, "Tell Darson I'll let him know what to do. Tell him that if he doesn't follow my orders, the little girl will die!"

Hannah pushed herself up on one elbow, trying to catch her own breath. She forced the pain she was feeling from her mind and concentrated on Natalie Ingram. "Please don't hurt Emily," she asked.

"Then tell Darson I mean business." Natalie backed up until she was beside Kendrick. He was still holding Emily, who was too frightened now to continue fighting. She stood still, gripped by his hard fist. Natalie reached behind the terrified girl and opened the door. "You stupid bitch," she said to Hannah. "You and Darson deserve each other. Too bad he's going to die first."

Hannah awkwardly got to her feet, her fear for Emily and Rory driving her. "What do you mean?" she demanded.

Natalie paid no attention to the question. "No one follows us, or the girl will die!" she said. Then, digging her fingers into Emily's shoulder, she dragged the girl out the door. Kendrick followed close behind them, still covering the four sisters with his pistol.

Before Hannah or the others could do anything else, the kidnappers and their hostage were gone, vanishing into the night.

Natalie felt a fierce exultation coursing through her as they hurried away from the Campbell house. All of the years she had allowed herself to be led by others seemed such a waste now. She was in charge of her own life . . . and anyone who got in her way would pay dearly.

"Natalie, why are we doing this?" Kendrick demanded as he looked worriedly over his shoulder. "This is all crazy!"

"No," she said flatly. "There is a good reason, Stefan. Just do as I say and get us some horses."

"But I'm no horse thief—"

"Do it, Stefan!" Her tone left no room for argument.

He picked out two animals tied to a hitch rail and jerked their reins loose. Awkwardly, he led them over to Natalie and Emily. "Will these do?"

Natalie nodded. She waited until Kendrick had mounted, and then she lifted up the little girl to him.

Emily finally got up the courage to speak again. "I—I'm going to scream," she threatened.

"You do and I'll cut your throat," Natalie said calmly. She slipped a small dagger from beneath her dress and held it so that Emily could see the blade. The girl pressed her lips tightly together.

As Natalie climbed into the saddle on the other horse, Kendrick said, "Look, we can still let the kid go and ride out of here. Darson's going to be looking for us. We can't afford to waste any more time." His face was coated with nervous sweat. He had come to Bonanza City to pull a

swindle on Odell Winborn, not to get involved in a
kidnapping.

Natalie ignored his words and swung her horse around,
kicking it into a gallop. She felt Kendrick's eyes on her
retreating back for a moment and then heard him spur on
his horse after her.

Just as Natalie had known he would.

She knew that the people on the street who were watching them ride out of town would be able to put Darson on
their trail. That was no problem, Natalie thought. She
intended to let him know exactly where they were. That
was all part of the plan.

They retraced the route she had taken the night before,
when she had gone to the Vista mine to plant the dynamite. Kendrick recognized the trail as they climbed into
the hills, and he urged his horse up next to Natalie's. "We
can't go to the mine!" he told her. "There'll be people
there!"

"Only a watchman," Natalie said over the beat of the
horses' hooves. "Everyone else is afraid of more cave-ins.
That fool Simmons told me!"

Kendrick was having trouble handling the horse and
holding Emily in the saddle in front of him at the same
time, but he managed to look over at Natalie and say,
"You really did cause the cave-in, didn't you?"

Her lips curved in a smile that was revealed by the
moonlight. "Of course. I told you I'd see to it that that
mine was worthless, and now it is."

"I ought to kill you."

"You won't," she said, with supreme confidence.

After a moment, she saw Kendrick shake his head. He
was not going to kill anyone, Natalie knew, unless it was
to protect her.

A lantern was burning inside one of the mine buildings
when they rode up. The door was open, and a man's shape
appeared there a moment later, drawn by the sound of
horses. The watchman peered out into the night, a shotgun cradled in his arms, and called, "Who's there?"

Natalie reined in, bringing her horse to a stop ten feet
from the open door. As Kendrick halted beside her, she

reached over, her hand snaking underneath his coat and finding the butt of his Smith & Wesson Number Two. She pulled the little pistol from its shoulder holster and pointed it at the incredulous watchman.

The man tried to bring his shotgun up, but Natalie pulled the trigger before he could. The flat crack of the pistol merged with Kendrick's surprised cry of protest as the bullet smacked into the watchman's forehead. Natalie could see the dark little hole it made as he dropped the shotgun and sagged backward, falling heavily.

"My God," Kendrick said softly.

"Not mine," Natalie said. "Not anymore. I serve only the darker lords now."

Wisely, Kendrick said nothing in reply. She would have killed him if he had mocked her beliefs again.

Natalie dismounted and led her horse toward the black mouth of the mine shaft. Kendrick followed her, keeping one hand firmly on Emily. If the little girl slipped away, they would have a devil of a time finding her in the shadows.

There was an unlit lantern hanging on a pole at the mine entrance. Getting a match from Kendrick and giving him back his gun, Natalie soon had the lantern burning and used it to light their way into the shaft. Fifty feet into the tunnel, she stopped and gestured at one of the heavy timbers supporting the roof. "Tie the girl to that," she ordered.

Kendrick did as he was told, binding the terrified Emily to the beam with a length of cord that Natalie had picked up outside the mine. When that was done, he sleeved sweat off his forehead and said, "Now will you tell me what this is all about, Natalie?"

"Of course. We're going to use our little hostage to trade for Sonora Pike."

Kendrick frowned. "Pike? What have we got to do with an outlaw like Sonora Pike?"

"He's my brother," Natalie replied quietly.

She told him then about her previous rescue attempt, the one that had failed when Rory Darson recaptured Pike and brought him back to Bonanza City. Kendrick stared at her as she explained everything that had happened since all of them had ridden in together on that stagecoach.

When she was done, he shook his head in bafflement and said, "You've been looking for him all of these years?"

"Ever since he left," Natalie replied. "I knew I'd find him someday."

"I guess I can understand that," Kendrick said slowly. "But why do you want to help him? I'd think you'd want to kill him!"

"He loved me."

"He *raped* you! You were only twelve years old, and he raped you! His own sister!"

"He loved me," Natalie repeated, her voice hushed, her eyes far away. Eyes that now, in the harsh yellow glare of the lantern, were almost totally mad.

Chapter Twelve

"He'll be all right," Dr. Madison told Rory as he washed his hands. The doctor's face was lined and weary. The last couple of days had been as long for him as for anyone else, and now he had been summoned to care for Vern Simmons's gunshot wound. "He lost quite a bit of blood, but the bullet missed anything important."

"Appreciate that, Doc," Rory said. "I hope I don't have any more business for you tonight."

Madison grunted. "You and me both, Sheriff."

Vern was bedded down in another of the hotel's rooms, near the room where the two injured miners were recuperating. He had regained consciousness while the doctor was tending his wound and had insisted at first that he was fine. Rory had had to hold him down for a moment until Vern realized just what bad shape he was in. Once the injury was cleaned and bandaged, Vern had refused the sleeping potion the doctor tried to give him.

Now, as Rory and the doctor left the room and returned to the hotel lobby, the front doors banged open and a distraught female figure rushed in.

"I just heard about Vern," Ellen Harwood said, fighting back tears. "H-how is he, Doctor?"

Madison patted her arm. "He's going to be just fine, Ellen. There's no permanent damage. He's probably still awake, so why don't you go on in and see him?" He pointed to the door of the room.

A smile of relief lit up Ellen's face as she listened to the doctor's encouraging words. "Thank you, Doctor!" she said breathlessly before hurrying to the door of Vern's room. Opening it without knocking, she disappeared inside.

After a moment, Rory said, "Is it just me, Doc, or is that gal in love with Vern?"

"It's not just you," Madison replied dryly. "Everyone in town knows except Vern. That young fool's too blind to see it." He snorted. "Maybe coming as close to dying as he did tonight will open up his eyes."

Rory turned toward the front doors of the hotel, his face grim. He still had to get on the trail of Kendrick and Natalie Ingram before it grew too cold. They had a lot of questions to answer.

Before he could take a step in that direction, another woman appeared in the doorway, tears streaming down her face, her eyes wide with horror, her long red hair disheveled and her clothes torn and ripped.

Rory stopped in his tracks. It was Hannah.

She saw him and plunged forward into his arms. Instinctively, he embraced her, and her body shook with hysterical sobs. Unsure of what to say, he held her tightly for a moment, patting her on the back with one of his big hands.

Beside him, the doctor thundered, "My God, Hannah, what's wrong?"

She took a deep breath, swallowing her sobs. She tried to speak once and could not manage it, but finally she said, "Emily . . . They've taken Emily!"

Rory stiffened in shock. The night was warm, but he suddenly felt cold. "Who?" he asked. "Who took her?"

"That . . . that woman . . . Natalie Ingram! She and her friend Mr. Kendrick!"

Kendrick again! The score was mounting, Rory thought bleakly. If they harmed that little girl, nothing would ever stop him from hunting them down.

With his hands on Hannah's shoulders, he leaned her back enough so that he could see her face. "Tell me what happened," he said flatly.

In a halting voice, Hannah explained how Natalie and Kendrick had arrived at the Campbell house and grabbed

Emily. "I . . . I tried to stop them, but I just couldn't," she said.

From the shape she was in, Rory guessed it had been quite a fracas. Keeping his voice calm and not letting his own worry take over, he said, "We'll get her back, Hannah. I promise you we'll get her back." Glancing over at the doctor, he went on, "Doc, can you take care of Hannah?"

"Of course," Madison replied, his own weariness seemingly forgotten. He slipped an arm around Hannah's shoulders and drew her away. "Come on, my dear. You need to sit down and try to relax."

Hannah clutched at Rory. "What are you going to do?" she asked, an edge of panic in her voice.

"Go after 'em," Rory said simply.

"Be careful," Hannah told him. "That woman, she said she wants to kill you!"

Rory pulled away from Hannah after assuring her that he would be fine, and he stalked out of the hotel, trying to block out the sound of her sobbing. There was no time to waste in consoling her. He had too much to do if he was going to bring Emily Campbell back safe and sound to her family.

Odell Winborn and the Vista mine were the keys to everything, he thought. It was time to pay another visit to Winborn, and this time the talk would have to be plainer.

Rory knocked on Winborn's door, rapping his knobby knuckles sharply against the panel. When that did not get any response, he doubled his fist and pounded on the door. A moment later, Winborn's voice came from inside. "What the devil is it?" the man demanded, sounding sleepy.

"It's the sheriff," Rory called. "Open up, Winborn."

Winborn stared at him as he opened the door. He was wearing a purple robe over his nightshirt, and his eyes were heavy with sleep and perhaps brandy. "What is it, Sheriff?" he asked. "I was asleep. It's been quite a long day, you know."

Rory nodded. "Reckon I know that. But there's been some more trouble, Mr. Winborn."

"Trouble at the mine?"

"No, here in town. I need to ask you some questions, and I need straight answers. There's no time to be polite about it."

Winborn frowned, looking slightly offended at Rory's tone. "In that case, I won't ask you in. But ask your questions anyway, Sheriff."

"Why were you going to hire Stefan Kendrick as the manager of your mine?"

Winborn hesitated. "Kendrick? Well, he has mining experience, and he seemed like such a bright young man, full of ambition—"

"It didn't have anything to do with Natalie Ingram?" Rory was guessing, but he had seen enough swindlers and confidence men throughout the West to know the way many of them operated.

"I was acquainted with Mr. Kendrick's cousin, of course," Winborn replied. "We all had dinner together several times."

"I rode in with them on the stage, and they didn't say anything about being related."

"Well . . . perhaps there was no reason for them to mention it." Winborn was beginning to look more disturbed. "Really, I don't see what this has to do with anything, Sheriff."

"You didn't have any kind of romance going with Miss Ingram?"

Even in the bad light on the porch of Winborn's house, Rory could see the mineowner flushing. "I . . . perhaps I had hopes that Miss Natalie might, ah, *like* me, but I assure you, Sheriff, nothing untoward ever happened between us."

The answer was evasive, but it was enough to confirm Rory's suspicions. It was likely that she and Kendrick had manipulated him into offering Kendrick the job. They must have had some sort of swindle in mind, because Rory would have bet all of the reward money he had ever earned that Kendrick was no mining expert.

But if that's the case, why the hell did they blow up the tunnel? Rory thought. He was convinced they were behind that, as well. He would worry about that when he caught up to them. "Thanks," he grunted, and he started to turn away, but Winborn reached out and caught his arm.

"What's wrong, Sheriff?" he demanded. "What's happened to Natalie and Kendrick?"

"Nothing yet," Rory said. "They kidnapped Emily Campbell a little while ago and took off with her. I'm trying to figure out what that has to do with whatever swindle they were trying to pull on you."

Winborn looked outraged. "I don't believe it! That sweet lady would have nothing to do with such villainy!"

"That sweet lady, as you call her, clouted Thaddeus Montrose on the head last night and stole some dynamite. I figure either she or Kendrick used it to cause the cave-in up at your mine."

Winborn's jaw dropped, and shock washed over his face. Obviously, he did not want to believe what he was hearing, but Rory's sincerity was undeniable. "You're sure of this?" Winborn asked.

"I'm sure."

"My lord . . . ," Winborn muttered. "I . . . I was such a fool."

"We all are sometimes," Rory snapped. He pulled away. Now that he had confirmed his suspicions, it was time to be riding.

There was only one other thing that had to be done first. Somebody had to tell Buck Campbell about Emily.

He detoured by the doctor's house on his way to the jail. No one answered his knock, but when he tried the door, it was unlocked. Madison was probably still over at the hotel with Hannah, Rory thought. He stepped into the house, went down the hall to the door of Buck Campbell's room, and rapped lightly on it.

The sheriff called gruffly, "Come on in."

Rory opened the door to find Buck Campbell sitting up in bed, reading by the light of a lantern. Campbell frowned when he saw Rory. "Thought you was the doc," he said. "Is there a problem, Darson?"

"Reckon there is, Buck," Rory replied slowly. "Emily's been kidnapped."

The dime novel slipped from Campbell's fingers as he stared at Rory. After a moment, he whispered, "Emily?"

"Far as we know, she's all right," Rory said. "She was grabbed just a little while ago by Kendrick and that Ingram woman. I'm on my way after them now."

Campbell threw back the covers and swung his legs out of bed, grimacing from the pain of his wound. "I'll ride with you," he said, his voice level and controlled. "I know this country around here."

Rory moved to the bedside and put a hand on Campbell's shoulder. "Hold on, Sheriff. You're in no shape to ride." He was cursing himself mentally. He should have realized that Campbell would react this way.

"It don't matter about me. For God's sake, man, she's my daughter!" Campbell's voice broke on the last word, as the stress of the news began to catch up to him.

"I'll bring her back, Buck," Rory said, repeating the promise he had made to Hannah. "Kendrick won't get away with it."

Campbell sank back, his face bleak. "Kendrick . . ." he muttered. "Something about that woman with him . . . Ingram, you said her name was? There's something about her I ought to remember . . ." Suddenly, his head jerked up and his startled gaze met Rory's. "She was there that night!" he exclaimed.

Rory leaned forward and asked, "Where?"

"In the jail. The night Pike escaped, the night he stabbed me—that Ingram woman was there! You jarred my memory, son, and now it's coming back. She came in with some crazy story about a prowler down at the hotel. I offered her some coffee and calmed her down, and then she left. After that . . . nothing! I can't recollect a thing."

Rory nodded. "She must have slipped something into your cup that knocked you out, then got back in somehow and let Pike loose. It's bothered me all along how he got out of that cell."

Campbell was shaking his head. "Reckon it could have happened, but why the hell would she do something like that?"

Rory grinned, but the expression was not pleasant. "Reckon I'll go ask Pike," he said.

He persuaded Campbell to stay in bed, although he could tell that the burly sheriff was itching to be up and doing something to help recover his daughter safely. As Rory stalked across the street toward the jail, he thought that he should have been out on the trail already, trying to track Emily's kidnappers. But his gut told him that he had almost all of the pieces of the puzzle now. If he could tie everything together by questioning Pike, he might be able to find Kendrick and Natalie a lot quicker than by trying to track them in the darkness.

Luke Warner let him in when he reached the jail, and the young deputy looked concerned when he saw the grim expression on Rory's face. "What's wrong, Sheriff?" he asked. "I heard some shootin' a little while ago, but I couldn't leave to check on it."

"You did the right thing to stay here, Luke," Rory assured him. He did not explain further but instead stalked to the door of the cellblock, unlocked it, and jerked it open.

Pike looked up from his bunk as the light from the office hit his face. "What the hell is it?" he demanded. "Can't a man get some sleep around here?"

Luke stared at Rory as the acting sheriff stuck the cell door key in the lock and twisted it. Pike sat up on the bunk, frowning in surprise as Rory yanked the door open and stepped into the cell, his hand gripping the butt of his Colt.

Pike started to stand up, but Rory planted a big hand in the middle of his chest and shoved him back hard against the stone wall of the jail. Rory slipped his gun from its holster and put the barrel under Pike's chin, pressing up with it so that the outlaw's head was painfully tilted back.

"Time for you and me to have a talk, Pike," Rory said, his voice deceptively quiet. "You tell me the truth, or I'll blow your goddamn head off."

"All right," Pike said after a second's hesitation. His voice was strained. "What do you want to know?"

"What's your connection with Stefan Kendrick and Natalie Ingram?"

"*Who?*"

Rory put more force behind the gun barrel. "That's not the right answer," he grated.

"I don't know what the devil you're talkin' about, Darson," Pike insisted. "You're crazy—"

In a flash of motion, Rory pulled the gun away from Pike's chin and slammed the side of his hand into the outlaw's wounded shoulder. Pike screamed in pain, but before he could do anything else, Rory had the Colt back against his throat, grinding the hard metal into his soft flesh.

"Reckon I've been getting lazy," Rory said. "I almost forgot the best way to deal with scum like you, Pike. I want to know where they took that little girl."

As tears of pain ran down his leathery cheeks, Pike gasped, "What little girl? I don't know what you're talkin' about!"

From the doorway of the cell, Luke Warner said tentatively, "I think he's tellin' the truth, Sheriff."

Through the anger that was gripping him, Rory realized that Luke might be partially right. There was a good chance Pike would not know where Kendrick and Natalie had taken Emily. As far as he knew, there had been no contact between Pike and either of the other two since Pike had been returned to his cell.

He took a deep breath. "All right. But I still want to know why Natalie Ingram helped you bust out of here." He drew back the hammer of the Colt. "And if you don't answer straight, I swear I'll kill you right now."

Pike was clutching at his injured shoulder with his good hand. Air rasped in his throat as he said, "She's my sister!"

Rory's finger quivered on the trigger of the gun as he considered Pike's answer. There was terror in Pike's eyes, and Rory suddenly knew that he was telling the truth. The outlaw was too scared to do anything else. Natalie really was Pike's sister, and that being the case, there was a chance that she and Kendrick had kidnapped Emily in hopes of using her to free Pike.

A few pieces were still missing, but Rory could see the big picture now. That did not put him a bit closer to rescuing Emily, however.

Someone knocked loudly on the office door. Rory backed up quickly, keeping his gun trained on Pike until he had the cell door closed and locked again. Then he nodded to Luke and said, "See who it is."

Luke went to the door and called out, asking the visitor what he wanted. A man's voice came back, "Got a message for the sheriff here."

When Rory nodded again, gesturing with the Colt toward the door, Luke unlocked it.

The man who stood on the boardwalk was medium sized, wearing dusty range clothes and carrying a battered hat in one hand. An envelope was in his other hand. The man had the appearance of a drifter.

He held out the envelope toward Luke. "You the sheriff?" he asked.

Luke shook his' head, and Rory stepped forward and said, "I'm Sheriff Darson. I'll take that."

"Sure thing, mister." The drifter handed over the message. "Hope it ain't bad news. I'm just passin' through these parts, but a feller stopped me on the trail and paid me five dollars to bring that to the sheriff in Bonanza City. I got the right town, don't I?"

"This is the right place," Rory said as he tore open the envelope and pulled out a folded piece of paper. His nerves were stretched wire-taut as he unfolded it and read the words written there. His face drew tense as their meaning sunk in.

From the still-open doorway, a voice asked, "What does it say, son?"

Rory glanced up in surprise to see Buck Campbell, dressed and armed, wearing his usual shell belt and holstered pistol. He was holding himself a bit stiffly, and his face was pale under his tan, but his eyes burned with anger and determination.

"I thought you were going to stay in bed," Rory said.

"Couldn't do it," Campbell said simply. "If you was a daddy, you'd understand. My little girl's somewhere out there in the night in bad trouble, and I can't lay in a damn bed and do nothing!" He pointed a blunt finger at the paper in Rory's hand. "That's a message from the kidnappers, isn't it?"

"Yeah. They say they'll trade Emily for Sonora Pike along with my word that nobody will come after them for forty-eight hours. I'm supposed to bring Pike up to the Vista mine by myself, tonight."

The drifter who had brought the message held up his hands and began to back toward the door. "I didn't have nothin' to do with this, Sheriff," he said earnestly. "I was ridin' along, mindin' my own business—"

Rory cut him off with a sharp gesture. "I know that, mister," he said. "Did you get your five dollars?"

"Sure did. The man who give me the message paid right up when I agreed to bring it into town."

"The saloons in this town have pretty good whiskey. Why don't you go spend it?"

The man's head bobbed up and down. "Yes, sir, believe I'll do just that." He disappeared through the door.

Rory, Campbell, and Luke looked at each other. After a long moment, Campbell said, "Reckon you know it's a trap."

Rory nodded. "I know. But I don't see what else I can do."

"They don't intend for you to leave that mine alive. You can't just walk in and let them kill you."

Rory met Campbell's level gaze. "I haven't had a family for a long time, Sheriff. I don't intend to see you lose any of yours just because I brought Pike here in the first place." He glanced over at Luke. "See that Pike's ready to ride in five minutes."

"Now wait just a minute—" Campbell began.

"I'm still the sheriff around here," Rory said sharply. Then he smiled and said, "Aren't I?"

Finally, Campbell nodded. "Reckon you are." His voice dropped. "Thanks, son."

Rory nodded but made no reply. While Luke was in the cellblock telling Pike to get his boots on, Rory unbuckled his belt and slipped off the sheath containing his knife. He slid the sheath down inside his boot and then pulled his pants leg over it. He had not been carrying the little Smith & Wesson .44 that he usually wore tucked in his belt because the weather had been too warm the last few days to wear a coat to conceal it. He would stop by the boardinghouse and get the gun before he left, he decided.

As Luke brought Pike into the office, the outlaw looked around and said, "What is this? Where are we goin'?" There was a smile on his lips, and Rory thought he already knew the answer to that question.

"Just keep your mouth shut," Rory said harshly. "Cuff him, Luke. In front, so he can ride."

Buck Campbell stepped to a rack on the wall and took down a shotgun. Breaking it open, he took shells from the desk and loaded it. As he snapped it shut, Campbell pointed the double barrels toward Pike and said, "Using this shotgun would probably bust open that wound you gave me, Pike, but I'll sure as Hades do it if you try anything. It'd be worth a little more bleeding to spread you all over the street."

Pike grinned. "Don't worry, old man. It looks like I'm gettin' out of here. I ain't gonna do anything stupid."

Luke hurried outside to get horses saddled for Rory and Pike, then joined Campbell in keeping the outlaw covered. With Campbell and Luke following behind to keep Pike moving, Rory led the two horses down the street toward the boardinghouse. Even though the hour was quite late by now, the little procession drew a lot of attention, more than Rory liked. The growing crowd of townspeople began to buzz with speculation when they saw Pike out of jail.

Rory paused at the boardinghouse long enough to run upstairs and get the little .44, which he tucked inside his shirt. A thorough search would find it, but he hoped Kendrick would not take that much time.

When he came downstairs, he found Hannah and Dr. Madison in the street, drawn by the commotion. The doctor was saying to Campbell, "I figured you'd sneaked out. You're going to kill yourself, you know that, don't you?"

"I'm fine," Campbell said gruffly. "Go peddle your pills somewhere else, Doc."

Madison shook his head, appearing not to take offense at Campbell's harsh words.

Hannah came over to Rory and put a hand on his arm. "You can't do this, Rory," she said fervently. "You know they plan to kill you once they've got Pike."

"Reckon they'll try," Rory murmured, "but I promised I'd bring Emily back, and that's what I intend to do."

Hannah's concern over Emily seemed to be at war with her fondness for Rory as she whispered, "Why? Why would you risk your life for my family?"

Despite all the hubbub around them, Rory felt at that moment as if he and Hannah were alone in the world. He could see the conflict in her eyes as she stared up at him. Slowly, he said, "I told you what happened to my family. I didn't tell you that when the raiders hit our farm I was off drinking and playing cards. Don't reckon it would have made any difference if I had been there, but I've always felt like part of it was my fault." He shook his head. "I'm not going to let your family down the way I did mine."

She bit her lip, tears glistening in her eyes, and then she rushed into his arms. As he hugged her tightly, she said, "I love you."

He took a deep breath, the scent of her hair filling his head, and said, "I love you, too, Hannah." Then he released her and turned to his horse, swinging up into the saddle, not looking at her.

Beside him, Pike also mounted up. The outlaw grinned cockily and said, "Looks like this is so long to Bonanza City, don't it, bounty hunter?"

Rory reached out, grabbed the reins of Pike's horse, and spurred his own horse into motion. The crowd fell back to let them pass, and Rory did not look back. His eyes were on the dark bulk of the mountains looming before them in the night.

Pike might not be returning to Bonanza City, Rory thought, but *he* would be. Back to Hannah and Buck Campbell and everything that had come to mean so much to him.

They were at the edge of town when two figures suddenly stepped into the street. With his arm in a sling and Ellen Harwood at his side, Vern Simmons said, "Wait a minute, Darson."

Rory reined in, not sure of what to expect from Vern. Like Buck Campbell, the deputy looked drained by his wound. He was cold sober now after his binge several hours earlier.

"What do you want?" Rory asked him.

"Reckon I've caused a lot of trouble for you, Darson," Vern said. "I wanted to say I'm sorry for that. I guess I had you wrong from the first."

Rory nodded. Vern's apology sounded sincere, and it meant more to Rory than he had time to show at the moment. "We all make mistakes," he said shortly.

"I want to come with you," Vern went on. "I can still handle a gun. I owe you a lot." He glanced at Ellen, who was watching him with a mixture of concern, approval, and love. "Until you came to town, I had some crazy idea that Hannah and I would get together someday. I didn't figure out until tonight who the right woman for me really is."

Ellen beamed with pleasure at the words. Rory nodded and said, "Thanks for the offer, Vern, but this is something I've got to do myself. The note from the kidnappers said for me and Pike to come alone." He leaned down slightly and extended his hand to Vern. "No hard feelings."

Vern returned the handshake. "No hard feelings."

Rory smiled at Ellen and touched the brim of his hat. Then he spurred his horse into motion again, leading Pike's along with him.

"Damn touchin' scene back there," Pike said sarcastically when they had left the town behind them. "The boy sounded like he was in love with that cow."

"You don't know a damn thing about love," Rory snapped.

And he knew that until he had come to Bonanza City, neither had he.

Finding the trail to the Vista was harder this time, since

Rory had no one to follow. He took his time, making sure that they were on the right path. Pike was full of threats and seemed to be enjoying himself now that his freedom was close at hand. He told Rory just what he was going to do to him when he got the chance. The details were brutal and savage.

Ignoring the outlaw, Rory kept his eyes open for an ambush, riveting his attention on the trail up ahead. Kendrick and Natalie could not be trusted not to make a move before they reached the mine.

Giving in to curiosity, he did talk to Pike long enough to ask him, "Why the hell would any woman do the things she's done for you, brother or no brother?"

Pike grinned. "Hell, Darson, she loves me. After all, I'm her big brother. Reckon she always looked up to me. I taught her all about life." He gave an ugly laugh. "Taught her about lovin', too."

Rory glanced over at him with slitted eyes. He muttered, "You bastard."

Pike laughed again. "Shoot, she loved it, bounty man. She was a little slut even back then. Took right to it. She was after me all the time to bed her. Reckon that's where I got my taste for young ones."

Rory spat in the dusty trail, but the bad taste remained in his mouth.

The sky was beginning to lighten in the east when Rory and Pike reached the Vista mine. The place appeared deserted, but as they drew closer, Rory saw a body sprawled on the ground near the mine office. Dismounting, he knelt beside the man and saw the bullet hole in the gray light. A watchman, more than likely, left up here by Winborn to keep an eye on the place.

As Rory straightened, someone suddenly called from the mouth of the tunnel. "Up here, Sheriff!" Rory recognized Stefan Kendrick's voice.

He slipped out his Colt and said to Pike, "Climb down from that horse, slow and easy. We've come this far. Maybe we can do this peaceful-like."

"Sure, Darson. Sure." Pike sounded as if being peaceful was the last thing on his mind.

They trudged up the hill to the shaft. When they were twenty feet away, Kendrick stepped out into view, a small pistol in his hand. "That's far enough," he snapped. "Drop the gun, Sheriff."

"Where's Emily?" Rory asked, still holding the weapon.

"She's inside with Natalie. She's all right, but she won't stay that way unless you do as I tell you."

Rory hesitated a moment longer, but there was no mistaking the menace in Kendrick's voice. Stooping slightly, he laid the Colt on the rocky ground.

"Tell him to get these cuffs off me," Pike called.

"You heard him." Kendrick gestured with his gun.

Rory unlocked the cuffs. As they fell off Pike's wrists, the outlaw rubbed the sore spots they had left, then suddenly stepped close to Rory. His hand darted out, yanked Rory's shirt aside, and grasped the Smith & Wesson. "You fooled me with a hidden gun before, bounty hunter," he growled as he scuttled backward, out of reach. "You won't get a chance to use it this time."

Rory bit back a curse. He had been hoping that Pike had forgotten about the time when Rory had first captured him. It had only been a few days before, but now it seemed like years in the past. So much had changed.

And some things had not. Sonora Pike was still a cold-blooded killer.

Keeping his voice cold and flat, Rory said to Kendrick, "I kept my end of the bargain. Where's the little girl?"

"Come on in," Kendrick said from the mouth of the tunnel. "She's been wanting to see you."

With Pike prodding him from behind with the .44, Rory stepped into the mine past Kendrick. He saw a lantern up ahead, and its glow revealed Natalie Ingram, standing in the tunnel holding Emily's upper arm. It might have been a trick of the light, but the Ingram woman's eyes seemed to have a strange glow about them. "Darson," she breathed.

"Rory!" Emily cried, her voice quavering with fear and pain and relief. She tore loose from Natalie and ran forward, throwing herself into Rory's arms. Natalie made no move to stop her.

Rory lifted the little girl, wrapping his arms around her and murmuring, "Are you all right, Emily?"

"I guess so. But I'm awful scared, Rory."

Rory glanced over her shoulder at Natalie Ingram's face. "So am I, sweetheart," he whispered.

Pike moved around Rory, joining Natalie and Kendrick in the lantern light. Still grinning, the outlaw lifted the gun and said, "Reckon that just about does it."

Rory knew what was coming. All he could do was shove Emily to the side and try to get his hands on the knife in his boot. It was a long chance, but it was the only one he had.

"*You bitch!*"

The bitter cry came from behind Rory. He twisted around, dropping to one side, as Odell Winborn stalked down the tunnel into the light, a gun in his hand.

"Don't move, any of you!" Winborn shouted, covering Pike, Natalie, and Kendrick. The gun shook as he pointed it at them, but not enough to lessen its threat. Taken by surprise, the trio stood still as Winborn went on in a voice that shook as much as the barrel of his pistol, "You tried to play me for a fool, Natalie!"

"You are a fool," the dark woman said coolly. "What are you doing up here, Odell?"

"I heard in town what you had done. This is my mine," Winborn blazed. "You may have ruined it, but it still belongs to me, and I won't let you use it for your vile purposes!" His voice softened. "Why did you do it, Natalie? I thought you cared for me. . . ."

Natalie laughed. The sound of it made Rory's skin crawl. Emily had her face buried against his chest as he stood against one wall of the shaft, between Winborn and the others. He started to slide toward Winborn, hoping to get Emily out of the mine before the shooting started.

"Care for you?" Natalie said, her laughter echoing through the tunnel. "I despise you, Odell! You're a worm, just like all men."

"You can't say that," Winborn rasped. Rory saw the mineowner's finger start to tighten on the trigger. "Don't say that, you whore!"

The gun blasted as Rory dove past Winborn, trying to get Emily out of the line of fire. As the mineowner fired, Kendrick cried out in alarm and leaped toward Natalie, his hand outstretched to push her to safety. Winborn's bullet thudded into Kendrick's chest, spinning him around and dropping him on the tunnel floor.

Pike snapped a shot toward the mineowner, his aim guided by years of experience. The slug caught Winborn in the belly, driving him back and doubling him over. The pistol slipped from his fingers as he clutched at his bloody midsection.

Rory saw Pike spinning toward him and instantly shoved Emily to the ground. The girl screamed as Pike jerked the trigger twice more, the gunshots deafening in the tunnel. Rory launched himself forward in a dive as the bullets whined past him. His fingers closed around the butt of the gun Winborn had dropped. As he landed heavily on the floor of the tunnel, he squeezed off two shots.

Both slugs smacked into Sonora Pike's chest. The outlaw was flung backward, bouncing off the rock wall and then pitching forward lifelessly. Justice had finally caught up with him.

Natalie Ingram stared at her brother's sprawled corpse and then dropped on her knees beside it. As Rory got to his feet, the thunder of the shots still booming in his ears, he saw her lips begin to move. She was making some sort of sign in the air with her hands as she swayed back and forth, and she kept saying something he could not make out.

Breaking from his momentary trance, Rory hurried to Emily's side and scooped her up. Her arms went around his neck, hugging him desperately, and as his hearing began to come back, he could understand her whispered plea to go home.

"Yes," he told her. "We'll go home."

She seemed to be all right. Rory checked the others. Winborn had collapsed in a bloody heap, his life rapidly draining out of him. Kendrick appeared to be dead, killed by the bullet to the heart.

And Pike was dead. There was no doubt about that.

Natalie continued her chanting. Rory could hear the words now, but they made no sense to him. He stepped toward her, intending to get her on her feet and out of the mine shaft. But then there was a deep-throated rumble from above, and Rory felt a vibration in the floor beneath his boots.

With a sudden, shocking realization, Rory knew what was about to happen. The gunshots had caused something to shift in the mass of rock above them. The Vista mine was about to cave in again.

There was no time to get Winborn out of the tunnel, no hope for him anyway, gut shot as he was. Rory reached for Natalie Ingram's arm. Urgently, he said, "Come on! We've got to get out of here!"

She sprang up as more rumbles rolled through the tunnel. Her hand slipped inside her dress and came out with a knife. Slashing at Rory, she mouthed incoherent curses. He dodged back, Emily still in his arms.

"I call on all the dark gods to blast this thrice-damned mortal out of existence!" Natalie howled, crouching next to Pike's body and fixing her insane stare on Rory. "I beseech thee, return the life to my brother and aid me in my vengeance!"

Rory did not wait to hear any more. Natalie was insane, and the place was about to come down around their ears. Already dust was filling the air, and small rocks were bouncing off his head and shoulders. The loudest rumble yet came as he turned and ran toward the entrance.

Behind him, still kneeling by her brother, Natalie Ingram screamed as her gods deserted her. Dust billowed through the shaft, enveloping her and the others. A split second later, several tons of rock crashed to the floor of the tunnel, sealing whatever good or evil was there forever.

Rory raced ahead, toward the mine entrance, staggering as more and more rocks pelted him. In his arms Emily shrieked, the screams abruptly cut off by coughing as the dust rolled over them.

The sun must have risen while they were inside the mine, for Rory could see the light ahead, marking the entrance, revealing the opening to the outside world and safety. Arching his back to protect Emily as much as possible, he kept running.

And he kept his eye on the light.

Everyone in Bonanza City heard the roar of the cave-in as the sun rose. Hannah cried out, and as Buck Campbell folded his oldest daughter into his arms, hope died on his own face. Vern Simmons, standing nearby, said, "I'm going up there!"

Other men agreed with him, and soon the town was a hotbed of activity as men saddled horses and got guns from their houses. Vern kissed Ellen Harwood before he swung up into the saddle, mounting somewhat awkwardly because of his wound. Then he turned the horse around, the other men falling in behind him as he started toward the edge of town.

He reined in a moment later, staring at the two figures riding slowly down the street on a single horse. The other members of the makeshift posse halted, a hush rapidly spreading over their excited, angry comments.

Holding Hannah against his broad chest, Campbell looked down the street, his eyes widening. Finally, in a choked voice, he said, "Honey, you . . . you better stop that crying and turn around."

Hannah lifted her head, saw the look on her father's face, and twisted to peer into the early morning sunshine. Swallowing hard, she said raggedly, "Oh, thank God!"

Rory Darson was riding into town with Emily in front of him on the saddle. They were covered with dust and grime, and a prettier sight none of the Campbells or the other townspeople had ever seen.

Hannah rushed down the street, the crowd parting to let her through. Buck Campbell and his other daughters followed more slowly. As Rory reined in, he gently handed Emily down to Hannah, and a tired smile spread across his battered face. "She's fine," he told her, "and I reckon I am, too."

He dismounted slowly, and he had never seen so many people shouting and clapping him on the back and shaking his hand. He was vaguely aware of Buck Campbell hugging him like a son and saying above the tumult, "Reckon you ought to keep that badge on permanent-like, mister."

Vern Simmons wrung his hand. "If you do, Rory, I'd be proud to be your deputy!" he exclaimed.

Rory's other arm had somehow wrapped itself around Hannah, and she was busy kissing him whenever she had the chance. Emily was in Hannah's arms, her fear gone, delighting in the celebration.

Rory caught Buck Campbell's eye and nodded. "I might just give it a try," he said, raising his voice to be heard over the shouts. His head was swimming. These folks seemed to have forgotten that he was a bounty hunter, a grim, hard man always on the move. A man whose life for years had been cold and bleak . . .

A man who, in Bonanza City, had finally found some warmth.

FIFTH ANNIVERSARY
SPECIAL EDITION

STAGECOACH

Station 36:

CASPER
by Hank Mitchum

Separated from her father at birth, twenty-two-year-old Amy Coaltree arrives in Casper, Wyoming, in spring of 1871 to meet her famous father, wealthy stage-line owner Ben Coaltree, for the first time. In the care of Wes DuMont, an employee of her father's, the spirited young woman enjoys her stay in the rough western town when Ben Coaltree is delayed. She especially enjoys the music and company of a man named Smith, the mysterious and attractive piano player in the Crystal Palace, a once-lavish saloon.

While Amy waits for her father's arrival, she watches as the Coaltree Cross-country Stage Line, represented by Wes DuMont, sets up business, intending to close down the local line run by the fair-minded Angus Hightower. When several unfortunate incidents happen to Hightower's company, questions arise about DuMont's method of competition.

Now uncertain about her father's character—or his business practices—Amy grows impatient as her wait continues. But her increasing fondness for Smith, whose exquisite piano playing gives a clue to his well-hidden past, makes the wait a pleasant one—until violence unmasks the truth about him and about several of the other people she has met.

Read CASPER, on sale July 1988 wherever Bantam paperbacks are sold.